Night Killer

DATE DUE

OCT 0 9 2006	

Also by Chad Merriman
in Large Print:

The Avengers
Blood on the Sun
Hard Country

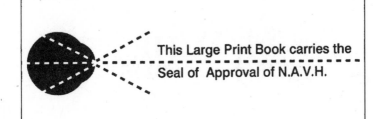

This Large Print Book carries the
Seal of Approval of N.A.V.H.

Night
Killer

Chad Merriman

WHEELER
PUBLISHING

Published in 2005 by arrangement with
Golden West Literary Agency.

Wheeler Large Print Western.

The text of this Large Print edition is unabridged.
Other aspects of the book may vary from the original edition.

Set in 16 pt. Plantin.

Printed in the United States on permanent paper.

Library of Congress Cataloging-in-Publication Data

Merriman, Chad.
    Night killer / by Chad Merriman.
       p. cm. — (Wheeler Publishing large print westerns)
    ISBN 1-59722-020-5 (lg. print : sc : alk. paper)
    1. Large type books. I. Title. II. Wheeler large print
western series.
    PS3553.H38N54 2005
    813′.54—dc22
                                           2005008686

Night
Killer

As the Founder/CEO of NAVH, the only national health agency solely devoted to those who, although not totally blind, have an eye disease which could lead to serious visual impairment, I am pleased to recognize Thorndike Press* as one of the leading publishers in the large print field.

Founded in 1954 in San Francisco to prepare large print textbooks for partially seeing children, NAVH became the pioneer and standard setting agency in the preparation of large type.

Today, those publishers who meet our standards carry the prestigious "Seal of Approval" indicating high quality large print. We are delighted that Thorndike Press is one of the publishers whose titles meet these standards. We are also pleased to recognize the significant contribution Thorndike Press is making in this important and growing field.

Lorraine H. Marchi, L.H.D.
Founder/CEO
NAVH

* Thorndike Press encompasses the following imprints: Thorndike, Wheeler, Walker and Large Print Press.

one

He arrived in Silver City behind a tag of steers some puncher was drifting up the canyon toward the town, apparently aiming for a slaughter house, yet he didn't notice the dust that sooted the late day heat. It was nothing to the shimmering wasteland he had been compelled to cross on foot, which would have killed him except for the anger that still drove him without rest. The obsession had made him insensitive even to the blood that pounded in his bandaged head, and the dried-out weariness of his rangy frame, and the parboiled feet in his worn-out boots.

At the edge of town the rider ahead turned the cattle into a gulch that angled off to the left but Hack Sumpter hardly noticed. He trudged on past a giant stage barn and yard and scuffed over a railed bridge and noted that, beyond the bridge, crowded street climbed on at the steep grade of the canyon. A descending, shabbier street snaked off to the left between the walls of weather stained buildings. It promised easier walking, which was the main reason he took it, although his immediate business was to find a doctor.

There was a wagonyard across the way, and the smell of burning coal, hot metal and singed horse hoof floated out the door of a blacksmith shop. Farther on, the street curved between the high, narrow buildings so typical of a western mining camp. Yet this was mainly a cowtown now, he knew. The bare plateau that supported the silver bearing mountain called War Eagle was carpeted by rich bunchgrass that had drawn drovers who stayed to establish ranches. Now the ranges ran practically to the city limits of the camp, and it was his knowing this that, originally, had drawn him here.

One of the structures ahead was a hotel labeled with big letters that said: WAR EAGLE, in honor of its setting. It had a long roofed porch with a row of round backed chairs along the wall, and they were all empty. He let out a windy sigh and sank into the first chair he came to, his head rocking forward when a dizzy wave hit him. In spite of hell and nearly no water, he had made it to Silver. Now, when he got fixed up, he had two men to deal with; if and when he found them.

When the vertigo passed and he opened

his eyes, a man was crossing the street toward him from the direction of the wagonyard. He came onto the near walk and seemed about to pass by when he glanced sharply at Hack. He stepped onto the porch and halted, looking down and not disguising the concern that had stopped him.

"Howdy," he said. Although a small man, his voice was like a trumpet. "If you don't mind me saying so, you seem to be in a mite of trouble."

"A trifle," Hack agreed, on a ragged breath. "Where's a doctor?"

"Doc Bethers is up the street, next block. I ain't exactly a nosy man, but it looks like somebody tried to blow your head off." His eyes traveled to the bloody rag beneath the brim of Hack's high perched hat.

"Somebody," Hack agreed. He pushed to his feet and could not suppress a groan. Sitting down had been a mistake, for his whole body rebelled against further action. The small man stepped forward and steadied him.

"I'll show you Doc's place," he said. "Where'd this happen?"

"When I was crossing the Bruneau. I lost my horses."

"Mean you hoofed it from the Bruneau across that God-forsaken country?"

9

"Nobody offered me a ride."

"Know who done it?"

"Nope, but I aim to find out."

"I wouldn't bet on it, friend. There's more kinds of scum runs the backcountry. We're too plagued far from the law."

"Got law here?" Hack asked.

"One marshal here in town. One sheriff and a deputy for the other ten thousand empty square miles."

Doc Bethers proved to be a young man whose office was in the street end of the little building where he lived. He came through the inner doorway as the outer door clicked shut and his glance sharpened on Hack. He said, "Howdy, Lundy," without even looking at Hack's escort.

"Howdy, Doc. Feller here forgot to duck," the small man answered.

"Gun shot?" Bethers asked Hack.

"Yeah."

"Well, you'd better lay down over there." The medico nodded toward a long, narrow table against the wall.

"Setting's fine," Hack said.

"Well, it's your wound that's going to hurt."

The bandage was glued to the gash when Bethers tried to cut it away, but he was gentle about it, putting something on it to

10

soak in and loosen the dried blood. When he looked at the red gash along the temple, he whistled. "Didn't this knock you out?"

"It knocked me out. From about four till after dark, the other night."

"He had to hoof it in," Lundy said, explaining the delay.

"I've got to clean and sew it up. You'd better lay down."

"This is fine."

The sting of the disinfectant and then the keen pricking of the needle were hardly noticeable in the thumping ache of his head. The doctor applied a clean bandage and went over to a basin to wash his hands.

"I have to report this to the sheriff," he said. He was wondering if that would make his patient uneasy.

"That's all right," Hack said. "I aim to see him myself."

"Lost your horse, eh?"

"And a packhorse with my outfit."

"Come far?"

"Texas. I brought up a herd."

"So you're another woolly Texan."

"Nope. I hail from Montana."

Bethers turned around, toweling his hands. "Where's the herd?"

"Sold it to Shoesole, over across the plateau."

The doctor's eyes sharpened. "Where's the money?"

"It was in my outfit. What they were after. Thirty thousand in gold. My profit on the deal."

"Another of them."

Hack got to his feet, his eyes narrowing on the man. "What do you mean? There's been more?"

"Several more. I happen to be coroner of this county. In the past three years I've officiated over five cattlemen who were carrying home beef money. You're the first they let live. See them?"

Hack shook his head. "Whanged me from under the trees when I rode up from the ford."

Bethers shrugged. "Well, you're lucky at that. I want to watch that wound. Besides, you're dried out, underfed, and you need rest. Get something to eat, then take a room and sleep a couple of days. Need money?"

He looked like he would lend it, and Hack began to like the man. "Thanks. I had a little paper money in a belt. They didn't think to look for it, I guess."

"Take him to Mrs. Nolan's, Lundy," Bethers said. "She'll know what to feed him and won't let him overeat."

"How much do I owe you?" Hack said.

"Pay me when I'm through with you. But I'd like your name."

"Hack Sumpter."

"Come back day after tomorrow."

Hack turned to the sidewalk with the diminutive Lundy, who said, "The courthouse is across the street, but in your shape I'd let the sheriff keep till I got some shut eye. If you never seen the bushwhackers, you ain't got anything new to tell him. Except, maybe, that the trail buzzards are still doing business at the same old stand."

"Where's Mrs. Nolan's?"

"Across the street from that porch you set down on. I live there. The rest of my name's Imes, in case you care. Been driving ore wagons around these mountains for twenty years. Come here when she opened, Sumpter, and this ain't nothing to the way things was then. You can stay at a hotel, if you'd rather, but if you aim to be around you'd like it better at Mrs. Nolan's. The beds're good and the grub's even better."

"Suits me," Hack said, "if she's got room."

"She needs the business. The mining's petering out, you see. Used to be thirty big producers going all at once. Now there's hardly a dozen. With the cowpokes we get, though, that's still enough to keep this town pretty hairy."

Hack had scarcely noticed the old two storey house, built on the square like most boarding houses, that stood across the ribbon of dust from the War Eagle hotel. They were nearing the gravelled path that led to the house when a horse and rider curved down from the street above. Hack recognized the animal as the one ridden by the puncher who had driven steers into camp ahead of him. The puncher came on toward them and stopped, and Hack saw a dark, powerfully built but inordinately ugly young man in the saddle.

"Howdy, Jim," Lundy said. "Light down and rest your calluses. This here's Hack Sumpter. He had a brush with road agents over on the Bruneau, and Doc just put a patch on his head. Shake hands with Jim Corbin, Hack. He nurses calves for Con Shea, out on Oxyoke. Coming in, Jim?"

"Only for a minute." Corbin swung out of the saddle and held forth his hand. His grip was strong and his eyes genial, although something in his homely face warned that he could spell trouble. He dropped the reins and tramped up the path with the others, his spurs jingling on the rocks.

"He's courtin' the daughter of the house," Lundy said, with an old friend's familiarity.

"Correct," Corbin said cheerfully, "and making headway backwards. What chance has a galoot who looks like me got against the competition?"

"Haven't seen the competition," Hack said tiredly, "but I sure wouldn't be any."

Corbin laughed. "Wouldn't want to bet on that till I've seen what's under that mane and all them whiskers."

"I've heard of Oxyoke. They buy a lot of Texas stuff."

"Used to. Been down a couple of times with 'em, myself. You hail from there?"

"Montana. Madison River country. Made a raise one night in a poker game and put it in Texas steers. Figured to make another killing and start my own spread around here."

Corbin glanced at the bandage. "Now you're back to taw."

"Except for a little paper money they didn't hunt for. Which I hope'll keep me going till I find 'em."

"If you do, you'll be the first who has. At least and lived to tell it."

Mrs. Nolan was busy serving supper to her boarders with the help of her daughter.

Lundy took Hack on to the back porch where they washed up. He must have signalled the proprietress, for she came out presently, a comfortably fleshy woman whose greying hair was wrapped around her head in coils. She seemed of two minds, when Lundy had explained, glad of an additional boarder but made dubious by the applicant's wild appearance.

"I want the loan of a wash tub and your wood shed," Hack said, "before I crawl between your clean sheets. Tomorrow I aim to buy me some clothes and find a barbershop. And see the sheriff voluntarily." He grinned at her.

She smiled back.

He was too tired to eat anything, and his head still felt like it had been split down the middle. The boarders were leaving the dining room when he went in with Lundy and sat down. Jim Corbin was at the table, not eating but drinking a cup of coffee and talking with the Nolan girl, who had sat down to her own supper. She was dark, slender as a willow whip and extremely pretty. Lundy introduced her as Mary, and Hack didn't wonder why Corbin had his eye on her or why there was plenty of competition.

Lundy pitched into the food on the table, and Mrs. Nolan brought Hack a bowl of beef soup. He was half through it when his head rocked forward, and he fell sound asleep in his chair. Afterward he was vaguely conscious of being helped across the room and up a stairway. Eventually he found something soft and comfortable under him, and he let go entirely.

He woke in broad daylight to find that the men had stripped and put him to bed. His headache was gone, and he was thirsty and hungry. He pushed to a sit on the edge of the bed, yawning and rubbing the back of his neck under the bandage and long hair he had grown on the trail. The clothes piled on the nearby chair were repulsively caked with dust, sweat and blotches of dried blood, but they had to do until he could buy more. His gun was still there, the belt looped over the back of the chair. When he lifted the pile of clothes he found his money belt, the contents intact.

That was his one piece of luck in the sorry outcome of the biggest venture of his life. He had carried expense money for his trail outfit in the form of greenbacks, and there was still nearly a thousand dollars of it left. All he expected to do with it, at present, was to pay his expenses until he found out what had happened to the gold that had been rolled up in his bedding.

The local citizens seemed doubtful about his chances, but maybe none of them had looked as hard as he aimed to.

He hadn't seen his assailants at the Bruneau, but he had a pretty good idea of their appearance. Coming up with the longhorns, he had followed the regular Ogallala trail to its end in Nebraska, then had turned west over the old wagon trail road to Oregon. They had reached Fort Hall, nearly at their destination, when a hard case rode into camp one morning. He had offered to guide the herd on to Shoesole range headquarters, high on the wild Owyhee plateau, for his meals. Since the country ahead was unknown to him, Hack had agreed. The man gave the name of Jones, and there was an off chance that he was leading them into a rustlers' ambush, so Hack had watched him closely. But nothing like that had developed, disarming him.

He was at Shoesole, tallying the herd and signing it over, when the man was joined by another rough looking individual. The two had left together, announcing their destination as Wells, the railroad town down on the Nevada side of the plateau. Hack was convinced now that they had laid low until he collected for the cattle and paid off his crew and headed out for Silver City alone. Fortunately he had asked Shoesole's range boss if he knew the pair. The man had not but he had seen them around Silver City.

So this seemed to be one of their haunts, if not their main hangout. Sooner or later they would show up here, for they assumed that he was as dead as the other cattlemen who had lost beef money in the same manner.

He walked to the water pitcher and drank from it, them began to dress. The regulars seemed to wash up on the back porch, so when he had pulled on his boots and buttoned his shirt he went down to the kitchen.

Only Mary was there, looking fresh and pretty, and he guessed that she was somewhere around twenty. She smiled and said, "Good morning. We expected you to sleep longer than that."

"I've got a good comeback." His eyes strayed to the clock on the window ledge. It was after ten.

She said, "You're too late for breakfast, but I'll fix you something in a jiffy. I expect you can have a full meal now."

"Thanks, but don't bother. I've got to go uptown, anyhow, and I'll eat somewhere up there."

"It's no bother."

He grinned at her. "To tell the truth, Miss Nolan, I won't feel comfortable around a lady till I've had a bath, some clean clothes and a shave. I'd also admire a haircut, but I don't reckon a barber could do much for me while I'm wearing this thing around my head."

She seemed in no hurry to get rid of him, even if he wasn't so elegant. "I'm sorry about your bad luck. Will you take a riding job?"

"Not right off."

"I know." She sighed. "The boys were talking about it after they put you to bed. I hope you find your men, but it's more than the sheriff's been able to do. He isn't even sure it's one gang doing all of it. At least there's no known gang operating around here, and there hasn't been for several years."

He deemed it best not to elaborate his own ideas about that. He said, "Well, a man can try," and walked on to the porch and washed up and combed such hair as showed above the bandage. He went back to his room for his money, gun and hat and left the house.

This street was called Washington, he noticed, and the one above it was Jordan, the main stem of the still busy town. The nesting canyon broadened here to accommodate the raw, frontier city of ten thousand miners, stockmen, business men and floaters. The business section skirted Jordan Creek, and the residential swept up the bald, brown hillsides on either hand.

The region was called the Owyhee because of the river that drained it and the whole vast plateau and the desert footing it on the west. The east, south and north faces of the plateau sent their drainage in tumbling streams into the Snake and Humboldt. The uplift lay where great, empty corners of Oregon and Idaho met the unsettled edge of Nevada, so that police jurisdiction was divided and skimpy, which created a favorite stomping ground for outlaws. It was no marvel, Hack knew, that the crime to which he had fallen victim was something of a local institution.

He found an eating house just up the street and had his breakfast, which sat easily on his stomach and informed him that he was over the worst of his reaction to the wound, which now had only to heal. Afterward he located a general mercantile and bought all the clothes he expected to need, a new hat and boots. Asking that the rest be sent over to the Nolan house, he carried a change with him and tramped along Jordan Street until he spotted a barber pole. He wanted a bath before he had the luxuriant trail growth of whiskers shaved off. He opened the barber's door and pulled up, straight and rigid muscled.

The shop was empty except for the barber and a man in the chair who was having his thick black thatch trimmed at the moment. Hack had seen the face above the snippings littered cloth before, very recently, for it belonged to the so called Jones. It was a hard, arrogant face, too puffy under the eyes and too cruel around the tobacco smeared mouth. It was not a lucky break, finding one of his men so soon, however. He had hoped that new clothes, a shave, the discarding of the bandage and a trim of his own wild hair would disguise him beyond their quick recognition. It was too late for that now. The heavy face stiffened, and the eyes went cold and wary. If lineaments were not sufficient evidence, the man proved his identity by straightening and shifting in the chair, as if expecting to have to defend himself then and there. He failed to speak the greeting that would have been natural if he was innocent, even though he was a long way from Wells.

Hack knew the best he could do was to

pretend no recognition, himself. He had more to accomplish than retaliation for what they had done. He had to locate this one's partner, and if there was a gang of them, he wanted to identify them all. Yet the pretense was not apt to be convincing to the man, either.

"Howdy," the barber said. "Be with you in a jiffy."

"Want to soak in your tub first," Hack said. It would be useless to follow the man out of here. He would have to gamble on the barber's being able to reveal something about him.

"Tank's full of hot water," the barber said. "There's towels back there."

"Fine." Hack went on through the inside doorway.

He bathed leisurely, giving the other customer plenty of time to get out of the shop. Then he dressed in his new clothes and rolled the old ones into a bundle he would tell the barber to burn. When he emerged, the barber, a pot bellied man with an oddly lean and houndlike face, was smoking a cigar in his chair. He sprang down and put the cigar on a ledge, and Hack got into the chair.

"That last customer," Hack said. "Struck me I knew him, but I'm danged if

23

I can place him. Who is he?"

"Monk Murname?" The barber laid the chair back. "He's around now and then. A bad hombre, in case that helps your recollection."

"I reckon not." Hack shrugged. "Never heard that name in my life."

The barber laughed. "That wouldn't prove nothing. He likely changes it pretty often."

two

The horse was lathered when it came over the rise and lined out on the downslope run toward the next ravine in this vast pattern of hollows and swells. The high country day was bright, with a red zinnia sun riding over the rocky wasteland that ran to the peaks of the Ruby mountains. The plateau's endless breeze flowed along the open slope and disturbed the sage and bunchgrass.

Far forward on the bare slope beyond the ravine huddled the surface works of a small and lonely mine. Old trailings showed that there once had been a large operation over there. The only sign of recent work, however, was a newer dump beneath a tramway that jutted over an incongruous stockade fence. The three-sided fence was a relic of days when Piutes and Bannacks preyed on lonely mines and ranchers, and its fourth side was a vertical bluff topped by a sharp lined rim. Lettering on the side of the largest building in the enclosure said: BIG CASINO MINING CO.

The hurrying rider followed a rough, rutted road that wound through the scabrock and desert growth from Silver City. He dipped his mount into the ravine, then up the far climb to the stockade gate. The gate was swung back at this early hour of the afternoon, but a tall, thin man stood just inside, with a bonehandled sixshooter riding loosely on his flat hip.

"What do you mean showing up in broad daylight, Monk?" the skinny individual said angrily.

Monk Murname pulled out a bandana and wiped his puffy face. "I got to see Spence. Somethin' slipped."

"What slipped?"

"I'll tell him."

Murname rode on into a compound that resembled the aboveground appurtenances of twoscore other mines, producing or abandoned, within three miles of Silver City. Activity signalled itself in the smoke and steam venting from various stacks and pipes on the roofs of the hoisting house and the small stamp mill operating at the foot of the grade. At that moment an ore car trundled out of the hoist works, pushed lazily by a man who looked more like a horse fancier than a miner, and ran out to the end of the cantilevered tram to drop a load of waste rock on the trailings. That looks real impressive, Murname thought as he reined in and swung down at the door of a small shack marked: OFFICE. He dropped reins and pushed open the door with a nervous shove.

A man sat at a desk across from him, working on a set of books. He was in his mid-thirties and held his well-knit body in disciplined erectness although he was lost in thought. He had a face women found attractive, framed by soft dark hair that tended to curl. He seemed a genial, well-bred man except to the discerning, who sometimes noticed a calculating light just under the surface of his brown eyes. He looked up at his leisure, but his frown was quick.

"You just come from Silver?" he said. His voice, a strong baritone, and his pleasing appearance might have made him a good actor, which in a way he was. "Haven't I told you —"

"Just a minute, Spence." Murname held up a hand. "I had to come pronto. That last one never cashed in. He's in Silver. I just seen him. Hack Sumpter, and no mistake."

"You chuckleheads!" Spence Lowell exploded. "Why didn't you make sure he was dead?"

"You kept tellin' us boys never to take chances on getting caught. So me and Ed grabbed his horses and got out of there some sudden. Hell, he looked like his head was blown open. Who'd have figured he could make it on, in that shape? Christ, it's forty miles."

"I gather that he did make it. Did he see you?"

Murname nodded. "And recognized me." He sighed. "He knows, all right. I reckon I could light my shuck, since I don't hang around your mine. But Ed's supposed to be your head man, and the people around here know that and him. No use in me knocking a hole in the skyline unless he does, too."

"I can spare you," Lowell said scornfully, "but not Ed Pointer."

Resentfully, Murname said, "Seems to me you let one get away once, yourself."

Lowell's eyes flashed. "I did something about it, too. This time you will."

"I did it for you that time, didn't I? What this time?"

"Nobody knows you have any connection with me, and you're supposed to be a fast gun. I've noticed you work pretty hard to make that apparent to people, too. So crowd Sumpter into a fight and kill him. Pronto."

"Now, look here," Murname blustered. "That jigger looks like a pretty tough man."

"Aren't you supposed to be? It's got to be you, Monk. And you'll stake your neck on whether you can make it look like self-defense. Whether you can or can't, you kill him within the next forty eight hours. Understand?"

"Why can't it be something like we did after you slipped?"

"An enemy as stubborn as Sumpter seems to be is an enemy I want dead quick." Lowell grinned thinly. "If you want to light your shuck, Monk, go ahead. But you'll do it without a payoff."

"Hell, I'll take care of him," Murname mumbled.

"So I thought. Don't take a chance on being seen leaving here. You smell like you spent the night with a Silver tart, so the sleep'll do you good. Get over to the bunkhouse and stay there till dark."

"I was in a barbershop."

Murname shuffled out, looking disturbed. Lowell closed the ledger he had been working on. Like everything else around here it was a dummy, anyway. He rose and walked to a window, more alarmed than he had let Murname see. He had to have more than security from the law. He had to retain his respectability, desired that almost as much as he lusted for money.

There was a woman involved, and he would kill Sumpter himself before he would let his chances with her be endangered. He had already had one scare of that kind, a horrible fright that had controlled him when he gave Murname his orders. He still did not like to think of the way he had retrieved the situation.

The thought of the woman was far more pleasant, and he leaned back, closing his eyes. He had been twenty-two when he hit Silver, a down at the heels young gentleman seeking his fortune in the West. The camp was at the height of its shrunken prosperity, but the discoveries, so everyone said, had already been made. His breath caught when he remembered the fabulous mines then operating on War Eagle: the Morning Star and Oro Fino, whose ore assayed $7000 in silver and $600 in gold to the ton, the Golden Chariot and the Poorman from which a solid mass of ruby silver crystals weighing 500 pounds was sent to the Paris Exposition to win a gold medal, the Ida Elmore and nearly thirty more. Big men had made up the picture then, mostly nabobs from the Comstock in Nevada.

There had been no room for impoverished gentility, or so they believed. And so he had come to think himself until one day, riding from Silver to the camp at South Mountain, he had found a curious piece of float. He had learned enough of mining practice to trace it to its source, which turned out to be a chimney of very rich silver ore begging to be mined. And he had mined it, opening it himself on a shoestring, borrowing where he could on the strength of his impressive assays but refusing to sell stock. And so was born the Big Casino, thirteen years ago this summer.

Lowell smiled when he remembered the three wonderful years of unbelievable prosperity. He could have sold the mine for a million dollars, then, perhaps more. Then, in the general plague or failure that hit the camp, the ore bottomed out. He had turned a large part of his earnings back into the mine already, but he could have quit then still possessed of a modest fortune. He had refused to quit, for he had built bigger dreams and could not relinquish them.

He had won himself a modest place in the local picture, and he had been one of the few to voice faith in Silver's future even while mine after mine was shutting down. He had backed his claims with his money, putting it into development work that slowly but inexorably bled him white. Then had come the bitter years, seven of them, that had made him a legend in some quarters and a joke in others, working on a shoestring again, borrowing until he could borrow no more, still trying to find the big bonanza he believed to be in his mine. When finally he was forced to admit defeat, he had admitted it only to himself.

The bonanza was there now, and he knew it beyond disputing. In two or three years he could retire to a fine Nob Hill home in San Francisco, as he had so long dreamed, and he would become the husband of the beautiful woman he had waited for for so long. Already he was shipping enough silver bullion so that no one was laughing at him, anymore.

He extracted a bottle from a desk drawer, tipped it to his lips and took a long pull. He shuddered as he hammered the cork back with the heel of his hand, and then he walked to the door and stepped outside. The wind had strengthened, picking up grits from the tramped yard, and he tilted his head while he walked across and entered the hoisting shed.

The engineer nodded, got off his stool and said, "You going below?"

"Yes."

Lowell stepped onto the skip and was lowered swiftly to the third level of the mine. A couple of lanterns lighted the gallery, showing the dark adits of the drifts running right and left. He took a lantern, turned to the right and walked for about a hundred yards, following a car track. Presently he came to another and larger gallery nearly choked by ancient waste rock which oldtime miners had dumped in there for riddance, to save hoisting costs. Two men were lazily shoveling the rock into an ore car.

"Where's Ed?" Lowell asked. He looked at Frank Lacey, whose mining labors had done nothing to reduce the fat padding his body. The other man was a bantam with a wizened face and darting eyes. Lowell could not care less about the mining proficiency of any of his men anymore. He had picked them with care, his yardstick being their nerve, ethics, and his ability to trust them.

Lacey said, "He left here a while ago. Thought he was going to your office, but maybe he went to the mill."

Lowell nodded, swung around and

tramped back along the drift. The skip had not moved, and he stepped onto it and tugged the signal cord. He was soon at the eye of the shaft and, without looking at the hoistman, passed out to the yard again.

Murname's horse had vanished, but since he was near the gate Lowell decided to make sure he had not left the compound in defiance. The lanky man he called to was Walt Yarbo, another in the hard core of his trusted lieutenants.

"Monk leave, Walt?"

"Turned in in the bunkhouse."

"Seen Ed?"

"Down at the mill."

Lowell walked on down the grade, seeing before him a rough structure about the size of a small barn. A trestle that carried car tracks connected its upper storey with the eye of the mine shaft hidden in the shaft house. The pounding of the mill's stamp battery loudened, and he could hear the blended swish of its steam power plant. He descended steps to a door at the lower level and went inside.

There were three men in sight, feeding worthless rock through the stamps and washing it over the amalgamation table. Lowell always got a twisted amusement from the fact that all this was essential, useless as it might seem. There were frequent passersby who saw the mine at a distance. Even more dangerous to him were the visitors, miners hunting work or the editor of Silver's weekly paper after news. These were treated courteously but never got into the mine or close enough to the stamps to see that what was being crushed was not ore.

He spotted Ed Pointer from behind for he was a short, blocky man who seemed to have no neck. Because of the racket of the battery, Pointer was unaware of him until he appeared at his side. Then the thick man turned hastily, lifting his eyebrows, never liking to be caught by surprise. Lowell had no special liking for him, but he was a good leader and could handle the hard cases attached to the new enterprise.

"You see Monk?" Lowell asked above the noise.

"Not since we got back from over east."

"Well, he's here. And your Hack Sumpter pigeon is still alive, in Silver, and aware that Monk's somewhere around here."

Pointer looked incredulous. "Sumpter? Stop kidding, Spence."

Lowell shook his head. "Monk's none too bright, but he wouldn't make a mistake about that. Apparently your bullet skidded off Sumpter's skull."

"It must be mighty thick. Besides — hell, that country should have killed him before he got out. You know it, rocky, short on water and no chance for grub at all."

"Well, he made it. Don't go to Silver till he's taken care of. If he recognizes you, too, the whole jig's up."

"Who's gonna take care of him?"

"Monk."

"I'd send Twitch Harper. He's got Monk beat a mile with a gun and he's a lot smarter."

Lowell smiled coldly. "I know that. I'm saving Twitch to use if Monk bites off more than he can chew."

He returned to his office, his uneasiness put down. If Sumpter was only average with a gun, Murname could handle him. If it proved otherwise, he would have to be a whizzer to beat Harper. And it was safe to use the twitchy little gunman. He was a known renegade and, by Lowell's orders, had never shown himself outside the compound since the night he rode in looking for a hideout. It was a lead pipe cinch Sumpter couldn't get around both of them.

three

The courthouse was across the street and two blocks south of Mrs. Nolan's boarding establishment. The man with the star listened with grave interest to what Hack told him. His name was Gilpin, and he looked surprisingly young and vigorous to have hair and a mustache as snowy white as his.

"I reckon you've learned that yours is an old story around here," he said wearily. "About the sixth time it's happened in the last few shipping seasons. The total take runs over a hundred thousand in gold."

Hack nodded. The shave, bath and clean clothes made him feel better and, he knew, gave him a more reassuring appearance. He had purposely omitted mention of Murname for he did not want the man locked up, at least not at present.

"I heard," he agreed. "But if I can get back my money or even my horses and outfit, I aim to. And I want it on record that I've got a right to them."

"We don't expect a man to do his own law work," Charlie Gilpin said, irritated.

37

"You can't imagine what we're up against. What's just one big country, as far as the residents go, is whacked into four political divisions. What happened to you was in my territory, Owyhee County, Idaho. A man was knocked off and robbed bringing beef money home from Elko, and that happened in Elko County, Nevada. Another coming home from Winnemucca was murdered in Humboldt County, Nevada, but had it happened a few miles closer home, it would have been in Baker County, Oregon. Figure what that does to law work. By the time us sheriffs can cut through red tape, the sign's cold, and we're all but helpless."

"Sure," Hack said. "I understand that."

Gilpin pointed a finger at him. "And another thing. I don't know when you cowmen are gonna get over your distrust of banks. You won't deal in anything but gold. The ones around here even bring it home and bury it in fruit jars. We had a case where the fella was killed in his bunk and the gold dug up before the dirt had settled on it."

Hack sighed. "I know. I just want you to make a note that I'm out to collect thirty thousand dollars, two horses and a pack outfit from somebody."

"I'll remember that at the inquest I'll

probably hold on you, Sumpter. But I wish you luck. If a single outfit's responsible for all the bloody work, I'd sure like to see it smashed no matter who gets the credit."

"If I smash it, I promise not to run against you next election."

Hack grinned, not wanting to leave Gilpin ruffled, and walked out to the street. It was well past noon and too late to eat at the boarding house again. He stepped into the restaurant next to the courthouse and had a meal. When he got back to his room he found his packages had been delivered and were on the bed. He put the new clothes away, then sat down at the window, wondering how he could get the jump on Monk Murname and learn who he was connected with here. One thing was apparent. He had to buy a good riding horse. He could try one of the livery stables, but a better prospect for a mount he would like was one of the ranchers around Silver. He remembered Jim Corbin, who apparently came in frequently to see Mary Nolan. He decided to see if Corbin could give him a good steer.

A knock on his door drew his head around. He called, "Come in," and the door opened, and he sprang to his feet when Mary came in.

She said, "You missed another meal."

He grinned. "But I'm here early for supper."

"I hope you won't mind," she said hesitantly, "but there's a boarder you haven't met who'd very much like to talk to you."

"Here?" She nodded. "Well, tell him to come in and see me."

"I think it would be better if you were the visitor," she said. "The room's just down the hall."

Puzzled, he followed her down the short upstairs hallway. She stopped at the door at its end, rapped, then opened the door. She went in and moved aside to let him pass. She closed the door.

Across the room by the window stood a girl as slender as Mary and with the same dark hair. Hack sucked in his breath. She was utterly beautiful, even with the white domino mask that covered her eyes. His brow knit in bewilderment while she stared at him through the slits, not seeming to move a muscle. What woman living needed to conceal her identity from him?

"I've brought Hack Sumpter, Shelby," Mary said. "Miss Shelby Michaels, Mr. Sumpter. My very good friend."

"Good of you to humor me, Mr. Sumpter." Shelby Michaels smiled and held out a hand. He walked forward and took it, mystified and pleasantly aware of her touch. "Mary told me about you this morning. After that I just had to see you. Talk with you, that is." She had a wonderful voice.

"Likely I'm easier to talk to than look at," Hack said.

"You're curious about the mask, so I'd better say at once why I changed that statement. I'm blind."

He stiffened. "I'm mighty sorry to hear it."

"Don't be," she said impatiently. "Just let me tell you how I got this way. It bears on what happened to you."

"Oh?"

"Please sit down. Are you staying, Mary?"

"If you'll excuse me, I've got work to do."

Mary left, and Hack took a straight-back chair while Shelby seated herself in the rocker by the window. She still seemed to be studying him through the slits in the mask.

"I was blinded a year ago," she said, "by a man who wanted to make sure I would never recognize him. That is, by his henchman. He and another man killed and robbed my father on the trail, the same as

41

you were robbed and left for dead. I saw them but managed to get away. Later a third man came to my door. When I opened it he threw something in my eyes. It was lye, Mr. Sumpter. I wear this mask because it covers the horrid scars."

Hack felt an uncontrollable rage come up in him. He managed to fight it down, but not very far. "You'd had a good look at them, apparently," he said.

She nodded. "They believed my father to be alone and weren't even masked. One was very stocky and not very tall. The other was tall and dark. Beyond that their faces were pretty ordinary and hard to describe. But certainly I'd have recognized them instantly if I'd seen them again."

"I thought they stalked their game. How'd it happen they didn't know you were around?"

"Our ranch was on Axle Creek. That's in Black Canyon, out on the Crow Hop plateau. They waited until dad was nearly home. I think that was to give them only a short distance to travel to reach their hideout. But it happened that I'd gone out to meet my father. I came on them just as they picked up his horses to leave. If I hadn't been mounted on a very fast horse, they would have caught me. But I reached

Silver and told Sheriff Gilpin, then went home to the ranch. The next morning I got the knock on the door."

"Wonder why they didn't kill you."

In a bitter voice, she said, "Perhaps it was chivalry."

"Was it much money?"

"I think they made a mistake about that," she said. "You see, my father trailed to Winnemucca with a made-up herd, acting as foreman. The others weren't ready to come back, but he did because I was alone on the ranch. The bandits thought the herd was all his, apparently, or that he was bringing back all the money. Actually they only got twelve thousand. Nothing like what you lost."

"You lost a lot more than I did, Miss Michaels," he said grimly. "That means they were new to the country or they would have known his situation and how close he was to home."

Shelby shook her head. "No, we were new then. My father drove his steers in from the Willamette Valley the fall before. I joined him in the spring. I knew no one in Silver, not even Mary at that time. But it did mean that I would be apt to run into them."

He nodded. "Somebody who is seen regularly around here. Any ideas?"

"Nothing definite. Jim Corbin and Mary have gone over everyone they could think of. The trouble is, the descriptions I can give are too vague. They fit a lot of people in general and nobody in particular."

Hack's anger still ate at him like an acid. A man who could disfigure a girl deserved worse than what the Indians meted out for punishment. "I take it you had to let the ranch go."

"I couldn't run it without eyes. Besides, I was in a Portland hospital for months while they tried to save my sight. It took money, and since then I've needed it to live. I sold the cattle we had left and leased the ranch and our range rights extending out from it."

He looked at her with sharpening interest. "You still own them?"

"Yes. I heard you expected to take up land here. I thought it might interest you to know the leases are expiring shortly, and I don't plan to renew them."

"It interests me. How many steers could it run?"

"Up to two thousand. That big enough?"

Ruefully, he said, "Too big for what I could handle now and not nearly as big as what I intended."

"Have you any money at all?"

"A little less than a thousand, and I've got to buy a horse."

"I still have a few thousand from the cattle sale and lease money. Jim Corbin wants to go in for himself, and he's saved up fifteen hundred. That would do it at Texas prices."

"But it's too late to bring anything more from there this year."

"I suppose," she said somberly. "But there's next year, and I've had some pretty good lessons in patience. Don't get me wrong, Mr. Sumpter, I didn't tell you all this for your sympathy. Even less to egg you into finding and punishing our mutual enemies. I'm happy here with the Nolans, but I want a useful life again. On the practical side, I've got to think about my living in the years ahead. I'd like to be a silent partner with you and Jim in a ranch. There's room out there to grow. You could get as big as you want."

"Does Jim know about this?"

"Yes. We talked it over last night. He can more than match your money and would like to throw in with you. I'd like to supply the rest, since that's about all I can do."

"I'm mighty grateful. When'll he be in again?"

"He brings beef to town from Oxyoke twice a week."

"Good. And one more thing about your trouble. Did you see the fellow who threw the lye? You haven't described him."

"I can. He was bigger than the men who killed my father. I particularly noticed that he was puffy around the eyes."

Murname, he thought.

He rose, walked to her and grasped her hands. His voice was ragged with tension. "Shelby, I know what it's like for you to be without sight. As to the rest, you're the most beautiful woman I ever saw or hope to see."

"As long as I wear this."

She pulled her hands free, reached up, and jerked on the thin ribbon that held the silk mask in place. He started to protest, not wanting to see what Murname had done to her, but the loosened mask came away and dangled in her hand as her shoulders stiffened. Her head came up, and she stared at him or seemed to stare through wide open and truly lovely eyes. He had to look close to see the faint tracings of scar tissue and the slightly inflamed-look of the flesh.

Gently, he said, "Why'd you do that, Shelby?"

"I had to. If we do what we talked about, we'll be together now and then. I want you to have no illusions about me. This is what I am, not what you saw until now. This is me."

"And a you with reason to be proud, Shelby. Why do you wear that thing? There's nothing to hide but a little redness that'll probably clear up in time. The eyes don't look damaged at all. They're beautiful."

"So Mary told you," she breathed. "She put you up to saying that."

"She did no such thing."

"Oh, it's almost gone away, Shelby!" she said, in a tone meant to mimic Mary. "It's cleared up miraculously these last few months! Poppycock, Hack Sumpter. She didn't see them when they were two pits of raw, swollen flesh."

"Did you?" he said.

She tossed her head. "I could tell. It's kindness on her part and yours, I know. Just the same, it's taking advantage of the fact that I can't see for myself." She tipped her head, and he saw her body tremble as she re-tied the mask that nothing could persuade her she did not need. But in another sense she needed it desperately, he realized, for it helped conceal the deeper hurt Murname had inflicted. She tried to smile, saying, "You didn't say if we've got a deal."

"We've got a deal."

He left, for the first time wanting to kill a man, yearning for it, and to make the dying as hard as he could manage. There were definitely higher-ups in this rotten game, and Murname wasn't going to lead him to them or to his money and horses, and there was no use laying off of him. As to the others, Shelby had narrowed the range in which to seek them. They were known around Silver, were passing as respectable citizens, and must be in some sort of legitimate business as a front for their outlawry.

He got his hat and left the house, restlessly driven, his patience at an end. At least a dozen major saloons still operated in the camp, and if Murname had not left town he would be apt to be in one of them eventually. He halted at the end of the gravel path, his gaze sweeping along Washington Street.

On his right was the big wagonyard where the freight outfits headquartered on this end of their long desert trek from Winnemucca, on the Central Pacific in Nevada. Across was the War Eagle hotel, and there was a stage office next to that, with a gambling establishment abutting the hotel on the other side. South of the depot was a drug store and then a shut up place Lundy Imes had called the Chinese joss house. In the next block were the courthouse and jail, and then a furniture store whose sign said it was also a funeral parlor.

He turned left along his own side of the street, passing a path that ran down to a footbridge over Jordan Creek. Beyond the path was the Owyhee Saloon, which he entered for a moment without finding his man. On beyond that was Sampson's Livery and then a T-shaped intersection where a steep street came down the hill to connect Washington and Jordan. There was nothing but a string of shacky buildings running on, so he turned up the hill to the main thoroughfare.

Jordan was lined with general stores, and every other door seemed to swing into a saloon. The Idaho and Eastman hotels were down from him, and between the two was the sign of the Wells Fargo office. There was a bank across from the express office, occupying a corner, and on the corner where Hack stood was the building housing the *Avalanche*, the town's lively newspaper. He started down his side of the street, entering each saloon for a look around.

When he had an encounter that produced something, it was different to what he expected. It was in the Pay Dirt, a quiet place because it ran no games of chance. It was almost empty at that afternoon hour except for the barkeep and three or four men standing along the mahogany. One stood especially apart, a thin, hunch shouldered man with grey hair and a nose that was sharp in profile. Some vague memory stirred in Hack, sufficiently strong to take him to a place at the bar, close enough for him to study the fellow. The apron came up, and he ordered a shot of whiskey, watching the grey man by means of the backbar mirror.

Suddenly he swung toward the man and said sharply, "Dunn — Dunn Hult!"

The man turned to stare at him with unfriendly eyes. "That mean something to you?" His voice was soft as a whisper.

Thrown completely off balance, Hack said, "Dunno. You ever hang out around Deer Lodge?"

"Maybe and maybe not. Why?"

"I've got a reason to ask, friend. You ever know a kid called Hack Sumpter?"

"Could be. Why?"

"I'm him."

The man turned slowly, some of the chill leaving his thin grey face. Hack had no idea how the tumblers would fall in his mind, considering the way they had parted those ten long years ago. After a study, the man made the thinnest of smiles.

"Yeah, you are." He held out his hand.

Hack laughed, his spirits lifting. "You're the last man I expected to run into here." Yet he was handicapped by not knowing just what it would be wise to say. They had been good friends when he was a kid, then Dunn had vanished without explanation or as much as a farewell.

"Likewise," Dunn said. "Let's drink on it."

Hack picked up the whiskey the bartender had placed at his elbow. They dipped their glasses to each other and emptied them.

"Going to be around?" Dunn asked.

"Aimed to settle somewhere around here. What're you doing?"

"Got a watchman's job at the Queen Bee. I'm on the swing shift and on my way to work right now."

"We'll be seeing each other, anyway."

"Sure. Still stickin' to cattle?"

Hack laughed. "More or less. Listen, Dunn. Do you know a smelly character they call Monk Murname?"

"Seen him around. Why?"

"I've got a score to settle. Seen him today?"

Dunn shook his head. "Not at all, lately. When he's around he hangs out in the Owyhee saloon. Tell you one thing for certain. Be careful of him." He tossed a coin on the counter. "Gotta leave. Be time to go to work by the time I get to the mine."

"We've got to get together and hash over old times, Dunn."

"Sure." Dunn nodded and walked out.

Hack ordered another drink. His thoughts had gone back to the time when he was sixteen and the nighthawk on the Iron Cross, where Dunn had been a top rider and a much more vigorous man than he had just now seemed. Dunn had cottoned to him, too, and then Hack's liking had blossomed into hero worship overnight. Dunn had outdrawn and killed a feared desperado on the streets of Deer Lodge in a display of speed and accuracy that had made him a local celebrity.

Hack grinned when he recalled how he had pestered Dunn to teach him to handle a gun the same way. It was to Dunn's credit that he had tried to talk him out of it, but finally he gave in. It turned out that he had a second Colt that matched the one he usually carried. One Sunday he slipped the spare into his saddlebag, and they rode out together. Well away from headquarters, Dunn had tacked a target to a tree. He showed Hack how the weapons were put together and talked a while about handling and using them properly. Then he emptied one gun into a bull's-eye no larger than a dollar and repeated the stunt with the gun in his left hand, something his other admirers had never seen him do. He reloaded and did it again, alternating shots between the two crashing pieces in what seemed one stretched out sound.

Hack had been dumbfounded, although there was nothing really show-off in the way Dunn had done it. Then, after explaining the fundamentals of target shooting, he handed a gun to Hack. By the time he called a halt, Hack was hot with frustration and shame, but Dunn seemed satisfied.

"Your left hand's no good," he said, "but your right's above average. That's all you need. The big thing's your frame of mind."

"What's that got to do with it?"

"Everything." Dunn looked at him with cold eyes. "Don't wait till you're in the bind to make your decision. Get it settled beforehand that if a man clearly aims to kill you, you're gonna kill him if you can.

The time you save can save your life and cost him his."

Dunn became a hard taskmaster in the Sunday after Sunday they spent in some lonely spot by themselves. Hack could not help being curious about his friend and the details of his life that he slurred over in a coldly guarded manner. Hack gave up trying to figure anything like that out, eventually, and the day came when his right hand was almost as good as Dunn's. Fortunately, he had never had to put the skill into use against a fellow man.

At the end of the fall roundup, that year, Dunn simply vanished into thin air without warning and without a word of leavetaking.

four

The last sun blazed on the peaks of War Eagle mountain, which wrapped around Silver City in a giant horseshoe and had provided the bonanza of silver that brought the town into being. The yawning canyon that ran down past Ruby City and Booneville and Wagontown already lay in twilight, and the last ore wagons were being unhitched for the night. From the incircling ranges cow punchers drifted into town to taste the high life that had abated but little since the roaring days of the boom.

The evening stage from Boise was unloading across the street from the Nolan house, and the busy racket of the nearby wagonyard had died away until another morning. Most of the boarders had left the big, box shaped house and drifted off to their various diversions. Lundy Imes had invited Hack to accompany him to Dutch Nick's, across the footbridge over Jordan Creek, which was a teamster hangout because Nick had handled a jerkline once himself.

Hack had declined the invitation for he had already gained something from his unexpected reunion with Dunn Hult. Dunn had said that the Owyhee Saloon, just a few doors up the street from the porch where Hack waited, was Monk Murname's town hangout. Hack sat thinking about Shelby Michaels. She had not joined the regulars for supper, and he supposed it was because eating was something of a problem for her in her unsighted state and she preferred to take her meals in private. He still raged at the animal ferocity of the man who had harmed her, and he was positive that the man was Murname.

He was drawn from his thoughts when a horse passing along the street angled in to the hitch ring in front of the house. The rider swung out of the saddle. He was tall, narrow at the hips and wide in the shoulders, and he wore California pants and polished boots. He tied the horse and came up the path toward the house. He glanced at Hack with sharpening interest as he ascended the steps and he nodded. His eyes fixed for a moment on the head bandage showing under Hack's Montana-peaked hat.

"Evening," he said, then crossed to the doorway and rapped lightly, like an old friend would.

Mary came to the door and pushed open the fly screen, which was all that was shut. She said pleasantly, "Good evening, Spence. How are you?"

"Fine, Mary. And you?"

"Equally." She stepped out. "It's hot indoors. Let's sit out here." Then she noticed Hack and seemed surprised that he had not drifted off like the other men. She added, "This is our new boarder, Spence. Mr. Sumpter, meet Mr. Lowell."

Lowell swung slowly as Hack got to his feet. He offered his hand with a curious expression on his face. "Glad to know you, Sumpter," he said. "Your hat and the bandage suggest you're the Montanan that was bushwhacked on the trail. A fellow was telling me about that uptown."

"I'm the one," Hack agreed. So this was Jim Corbin's competition for Mary. He wondered if that was the reason he felt an instinctive dislike of the man.

"Get a look at them?" Lowell asked.

Hack shook his head. "It was what you said — a bush-whack."

"Well, there's been too much of that."

"We see alike there." Hack started toward the steps.

Quickly, Mary said, "Don't go. We didn't intend to run you off."

Hack smiled. "My throat was dry, and I was about to remedy it, anyhow. See you again, Lowell." He descended the steps and went down the path to the street.

He walked on to the Owyhee saloon, which proved to hold a crowd of miners, millhands, and punchers in from the ranges. The long, high bar was jammed elbow to elbow, and talk rolled into an unintelligible rumble that bounced off the smudgy walls. Monk Murname was not in sight. Hack had his drink, then walked over to the benches running along the wall opposite the bar. He picked up a copy of the *Avalanche* that lay there and sat down. Nobody paid any attention to him, and he watched night blacken the window panes.

Some of the patrons seemed set for the night and others drifted in and out. He examined each new face with what he tried to make a sweeping and casual interest. After an hour of this the door burst open, and Murname strode in, ploughing toward the bar and shoving men aside with his wide shoulders. The way they permitted it without open resentment indicated the reputation he had made here. A space for him cleared at the bar, and Murname demanded whiskey in a voice that filled the hushed room.

"The bullyboy's in a mean mood to-night," somebody near Hack murmured.

Hack noticed that Murname wore his sixshooter on his left hip, reversed for a cross draw. His presence had turned the whole crowd edgy, and Hack put down the newspaper, rose and walked to the open space on Murname's left, coming in much closer than he needed to be. His eyes locked with the man's in the backbar mirror. Murname was raising a shot glass. It halted halfway to his mouth while he stared at the mirror. Then he tossed off the drink and put the glass down. Neither man spoke, for ostensibly they were strangers.

The bartender came up hesitantly. The crowd was watching in tight silence. "What'll it be?" the apron asked, plainly nervous.

"Never mind," Hack said.

The man shuffled off in relief, and Murname's face broke into a scowl. He had not been certain until then that he was being baited. Used to having it the other way, evidently, he hesitated and tried to figure it out.

"So you don't remember me," Hack murmured.

"Seen you in the barber shop, this morning. Remember that rag on your head." He seemed to hope his shave and haircut had changed his appearance enough to make Hack uncertain.

"Farther back than that."

"Look — !"

Murname started to swing and face him, but Hack's hand stabbed out. It caught the grips of Murname's reversed gun so that it jerked free of the leather on the man's own hasty back pull. Hack's arm flicked, and the sixshooter landed in the sawdust behind the bar. Murname's eyes shot desperately to Hack's hip, and he let out a gusty relief when he saw no weapon.

"What's the meaning of this?" he demanded.

"Aim to see how tough you are without that hogleg."

"Who are you?" Murname said hotly, trying to keep up his feeble pretense, at least for the sake of the crowd.

"Call me a friend of Miss Shelby Michaels, right now. However, there is more I could mention. I think you know that."

Murname's eyes widened. "You tricky bastard. If you've got something to settle with me, get yourself a gun and I'll get mine back."

His eyes heated as he made the challenge, and Hack knew he would welcome such a chance to remove the danger to himself. "He's leaking it, boys," Hack called to the intent watchers. "You'll smell it plain in a minute."

That was more than Murname could take. He let out a roar and rolled forward, scooping up a blow that, had it landed, would have cracked Hack's neck. But the tall body swayed aside, and the swing carried Murname into a punch that snapped back his own head. He reeled off, hit the bar with his back and found himself pinned there by a battery of jolting fists.

He weathered the blows with brute stamina until he could crook a knee. His kick, when he lashed out, caught Hack in the belly and sent him careening backward into a card table. Murname followed with a colliding rush that toppled Hack to the sawdust, and the larger man came down on top of him. "By God," Murname said on a ragged breath, "I'm gonna gouge your eyes out."

"Why not lye again, Murname?"

Murname's meaty thighs were pinned across Hack's chest, and his weight was too great to throw off. Hack felt raking fingers dig across his eyelids and jerked his head from side to side. Abruptly he bridged his back, gave an extra buck, and crawled out through Murname's crotch while the man rolled over his head.

He was up instantly, his shirt nearly torn off and sweat dripping from his face. Murname had ended in a sit with his back to him and shook his head and blew his nostrils free of sawdust. The bartender had grabbed a bung starter but had gone no further toward interfering. A ring of absorbed faces ran all around the central figures.

Murname sprang to his feet and lurched around, and his wild eyes came to rest on Hack. He advanced with his hands set like a wrestler's, for he had discovered the advantage of his weight and brute strength. Hack stepped away and, when Murname sprang, caught a hand in both his own. He wheeled so suddenly and so powerfully that Murname whipped out to arm's length, like a weight on a whirling string. The big man took half a dozen speeding steps before Hack let go, then he crashed head on into the bar and dropped to his knees, whimpering.

"My God," somebody said in a tight voice. "The cowpoke's too much for him, even with his head in a sling."

Murname refused to acknowledge inferiority. His eyes were glazed when he climbed drunkenly to his feet, and he had trouble getting them in focus. His nose had taken part of the collision, and blood streamed from it and dripped from his chin. He blubbered something incoherent, located his man and surged forward. His hand flashed out, and concealed sawdust hit Hack full in the face and eyes. Murname came in behind it, and his big fists chopped hard and short.

Hack pulled away. Murname's hammering seemed to paralyze him, to destroy his capacity to think. He quit trying to dig his eyes clear, and his hands found the man's slippery head. He bent his own head forward and jerked Murname's face against his forehead in repeated impacts that sent pain streaking through his own brain. It brought a groan from Murname and stopped his killing punches, then the big man back pedaled and broke off.

When Hack got his eyes opened, Murname stood with his hands pressed to his face, sobbing for breath. Hack slid in and hit him under the breast bone and made the arms drop. He hit him under the chin, once, twice and then again before Murname's legs broke at the knees and he collapsed with glazing eyes.

Somebody shouted, "Finish it, cowboy,

or he'll waylay and murder you!"

Hack stood waiting for the man to get up. Murname only groaned and rolled his head from side to side, then presently he pushed up on his arms and let his sick eyes stare at Hack.

"You yellow bastard," he said in a broken voice. "You're scared to fight like a man — with a gun." He dropped his head, used both hands to wipe his bloody face, then looked up again. "By God, I'll make you meet me — or run."

Hack's soft voice fell across the silence, "So you can fight that way. I figured you did your shooting from a rimrock." He found his hat and left the saloon.

He had gained little but satisfaction for what the man had done to Shelby. And as the surging drives subsided, he realized he had come to the spot Dunn had talked about, where he would have to kill or be killed. The thought rang with each strike of his heels as he went to his room, fortunately meeting no one.

He stripped off the tattered shirt and washed his smeary face. His wound ached and throbbed, as did the whole front of his battered chest, and his belly muscles were knotted. His lips were swollen, but his hands were not hurt. He crawled wearily into bed. It came to him finally that Murname would have tried again to kill him, anyway. The fight had forced him to make an open affair of it where, otherwise, it would probably have been by treachery. So he had best be met as soon as possible or he would set his own time and place.

A rap on the door roused him out of restless sleep, and he opened his hot eyes to the light of a new day. He ignored the summons for a moment, gathering his thoughts, then he called, "Who is it?"

"Me — Dunn Hult."

Hack got lamely out of bed, threw open the door, and the thin grey man stood there, looking at him with veiled eyes. "Come in, Dunn," Hack said puzzledly. Dunn entered the room, and when he had closed the door Hack turned to see the man surveying the marks the fight had left on him.

"So you found Murname," Dunn said.

"How'd you hear about it?"

"Stopped in for a drink when I come off work at midnight. They tell me you worked him over proper. How'd you pull his fangs?"

"Caught him off guard." Hack motioned toward a chair. "Set down, Dunn."

"Only aim to stay a minute. Hear he figures to make you shoot it out."

"So he said." Hack couldn't understand Dunn's concern. "You think he can beat me?"

"He's killed a lot of men. He's got a reputation. Maybe he can kill you, too. He seems to figure so. But even if you kill him you'll still be in trouble. You'll have a crown somebody'll be trying to knock off till somebody does."

Exasperated, Hack said, "Look, Dunn. I can still hear you telling me to kill the man who aims to put me under the ground. Murname sure does. I know enough about him he'd be more comfortable with me dead. There's men behind him, somewhere around here. Maybe they're more anxious than he is to see me out of the way. It could be he's got orders to kill me and quick, one way or another. And my bet's to meet him in the open while he's giving me the chance. It's the last one he would give me."

"I figured he was the one that bushwhacked you," Dunn reflected.

"Him and another fellow." Hack went on to tell what he had experienced and why he thought some supposedly honest men were back of that and the similar incidents of the past three years.

"You're in more of a bind than I

thought," Dunn said. "I figured it was just the two of you, and I felt responsible for giving you maybe too much confidence in your shooting iron. It's a bad thing to have."

"Speaking from experience?"

"Leave it this way. I'm ten years older than when I coached you on the Iron Cross. If I had it to do over, I wouldn't have let you talk me into it. A good gun hand can suck a man into things he'd step wide of, otherwise." He walked to the door, looked back to say, "Good luck," and left.

Hack dressed, strapped his gun belt about his lean waist, adjusted the weight on his hip, clamped on his hat and tramped down the stairs into the warming outdoors. He was cool and resolute, determined to show himself on the streets immediately, armed and ready, giving Murname his opportunity. It was his best chance to survive.

He walked up curving Washington to the bridge on Jordan Street, then covered the length of Jordan, seeing excitement ripple ahead and follow him. At the head of Jordan he stepped into an eating house for his breakfast, knowing that someone would get word to Murname. He had flapjacks and coffee and was surprised that he could eat with appetite. He paid for the meal and stepped back into the street, now bright with morning sun. It was still crowded, which it would not be if Murname had put in an appearance. He went all the way down to the bridge again, watched curiously but unchallenged. He felt let down, and wondered if Murname was up and around yet; when he curved down Washington, returning to the boarding house. He would have to try it again in a couple of hours.

When he came around the bend in the street he saw it was deserted on ahead except for one man who stood in the next block, on the opposite walk and facing his way. His throat tensed, and blood began to pound in his lungs. The man started toward him, and he was Monk Murname. Abruptly Hack saw that he had been maneuvered into a disadvantage. Murname had expected him to go back to the boarding house after prowling the main street without results. He had placed himself here with the dazzling sun on past him, so it would be in Hack's eyes. His cunning and treachery were at work even now.

He was close to the corner of the next street coming down from Jordan. The

Masons' hall was on beyond him, with a low building stretching from it this way. A blacksmith shop and some other buildings filled the intervening space. Hack crossed the street at the corner of the courthouse and turned down toward the creek. By coming in on the man along the stream behind the buildings, he could get the bright light out of his eyes. He could force on Murname the burden of spotting and meeting him, instead of having it the other way around.

Gun in hand, he walked swiftly, passing behind the structures, which were then on his right. Through the rear door of the blacksmith shop he saw several men huddled near the front wall. They were waiting and listening, aware of what was developing, and they intended to be out of the way of flying bullets. He passed the corner of that building and looked through the slot between it and the next structure south. The space was empty. He sucked in a long breath then walked into the slot, step by slow step. He reached the board walk to find that Murname had disappeared. Hack pulled in another breath, bewildered and exposed dangerously.

"Look out!" a voice yelled raggedly. It came from a man watching through a crack in the blacksmith shop wall.

The crack of a gun echoed the shout and sent Hack headlong onto the hot, splintered planks. Mistaking the fall for a hit, Murname sprang around the corner, his gun spitting gashes of red flame. Hack whipped up his gun and shot just once, and Murname went down in a knee-sprung spill at the corner.

"Hold it!"

Two men came clumping out of the jail office under the nearby courthouse, each carrying a shotgun; the town marshal and a deputy, energized by Murname's first shot. Others poured from opening doors along the street, and the men who had been in the blacksmith shop arrived first. Hack climbed to his feet just as the lawmen came up, their shotguns covering him.

"Hell, Bales!" a man yelled angrily. "Murname tried to murder him! Four of us seen it!" He looked at Hack in sheer disbelief. "Ain't you hit?"

Hack shook his head. Four bullets had dug into the boards where he had lain, but he was unhurt. His one bullet had drilled through Murname's heart, the result of the many hours of practice under Dunn's tutelage. That struck him only as an impersonal fact of grim and forbidding finality, but it seemed to have inspired an awed admiration in the watchers, just as he had once seen men grow that way about Dunn, just as he had felt toward the man himself after that long ago gunfight in Deer Lodge.

Bales, the town marshal, had grown vinegary from his years of trying to enforce the law where it was only partly wanted. Hack had seen the deputy in Sheriff Gilpin's office but did not know his name. The two drew apart and talked for a moment, then called him over.

"We ain't locking you up unless something develops at the inquest," Bales said. "But don't leave town."

"I won't."

Hack walked away, sickened and dizzy, although he could not have done it differently. Murname had cheated at every move. If it had not happened as it did, it would have taken place under circumstances where the man could not help winning. Yet only a while ago Dunn had warned him of a grim and inevitable aftermath.

It was only midmorning, although it seemed to him that the day was much older than that. He wanted a horse under him, to get out in the country and breathe its clean air and let it blow the ugly impressions from his mind. But he had promised not to leave camp until the inquest had either cleared him or put him in trouble with the law. If he hung around the loitering spots about town he would draw the sensation lovers. Yet he hated to go back to the boarding house, had the edgy feeling that he had somehow separated himself from the people there who seemed to have the makings of friends.

He might have foreseen that the excitement had travelled ahead of him. When he came in sight of the house, he saw Mary and her mother standing in the yard, staring toward him, their hands shading their eyes. They had heard the shots and rushing people on the street. It was too late to turn off, so he went on toward them.

"Who was it?" Mary asked when he came up.

"Fellow name of Murname."

"And who else?"

"Me. I had to kill him."

Her eyes rounded as she stared at his battered face, seeing it for the first time since the fist fight. He saw her cheeks grow chalky. Mrs. Nolan was frowning.

"But why?" Mary gasped. "Was he one of the men who — ?"

"He was one of them."

"Is that how you meant to deal with them?"

He stared at her a moment, then went on, knowing he had shocked her deeply and had much the same effect on her mother. His room was hot when he entered it, even with the windows open. He tossed his hat on the bed and sat down to roll a cigarette. The reaction was growing stronger. He could feel it in the dull ache in the back of his head and the nettling irritability that had oozed all through him.

five

The inquest was held the next morning and, in spite of Hack's uneasiness, turned out to be a formality. Murname's record in Silver had been bad. While Hack had crowded the fight in the saloon, it was because Murname made a practice of shoving people out of his way. Murname had made the gun talk even before a blow was struck, repeating it after he had been whipped and putting it in such a way no self-respecting man would dodge him. Witness after witness attested to this and to Murname's treachery during the gunfight, and the jury responded with a quick verdict of self-defense.

Hack avoided the outthrust hands and left the courthouse, crossing the street and going on to Sampson's livery barn. He asked for a rental horse. The stableman said, "Sure, but say, if you're lookin' for a good buy, I've got one."

Hack doubted that but told the man he'd take a look. The horse was in the corral in back and, to Hack's surprise, turned out to be a sleek black gelding with excellent lines.

"Feller just brought him in," the hostler said. "Would you believe that boy's run outdoors every winter?"

"You mean he rustled and come through looking like that?"

The man laughed. "That's what makes this fine stock country, Sumpter. There's hundreds of miles of bunchgrass, and plenty of browse that grows too tall for the snow to bury it. This boy grew up on white sage winters and bunchgrass summers. He wouldn't know what oats and barley look like."

"How much?"

"I got him cheap, and I'll turn him cheap. Hundred-fifty, rigged with a good saddle and bridle."

"How about trying him?"

"Sure, but you don't need to worry. Climb aboard and drop a hint, and he'll take you there."

Hack rode the horse through town then made a run down the canyon and back. He knew he had found what he wanted and went back to the livery and closed the deal. When he had paid for the horse and got a bill of sale, he again headed down the canyon.

He was thinking of Murname's companion, whom he had not seen in Silver

City. There were other camps nearby, all but ghosted now, but there was a chance he was hanging out in one of them. If he had not been in contact with Murname, there was a possibility that he would not recognize the man he had supposedly helped murder. If he could take this one by surprise, Hack reflected, he might learn more than he had derived from the fore-warned Murname.

Ruby City was only a mile below Silver, a huddle of decaying buildings showing life only in a hotel for passersby and a saloon catering to the same transients and the persistent prospectors who poked around the old, once profitable claims. On below was Booneville, in much the same state, then came Wagontown. They each had saloons and eating houses, but in none of them did he see his man. South Mountain was farthest away and quite a ride. A glance at the sun told him he could make it there and back by dark, for the black was a fast stepper with plenty of bottom. He rode on.

He reached the last camp in midafternoon to find a drab, sun-bleached town kept alive by a couple of mines still producing. He looked around fruitlessly, got a meal, and decided to take a shortcut up Boulder

Creek on his return to Silver, going directly over War Eagle Mountain. He still had a long ride but did not hurry for there were four or five hours left of daylight.

The country grew rougher at once, blending into the breaks that lay higher on the plateau; gouged and barren country that seemed to have been abandoned by its creator when only half finished. The trail climbed, with War Eagle rearing on his left. Presently the trail shelved to the rim of a canyon, and when he topped out he stopped to let his horse blow, dismounting and walking to the edge of the bluff.

His interest sharpened when, directly below him, he saw a horse and rider moving along the rocky, wall-hugged edge of the creek. He was puzzling as to why the fellow had left the trail when the horse stopped, and the rider all but fell from the saddle. The man stood there a moment, clinging to the saddle horn for balance, then he went staggering to the water and pulled off his shirt. Hack's eyes narrowed, for the upper part of the fellow's arm was bandaged. He began to unwind the cloth, slow and clumsy with it. Finally he soaked it in the creek water and began to rewrap it around the arm which hung uselessly. Presently he laid back on the rocks, the picture of utter exhaustion.

He was hurt and, wanting to know more about it, Hack stepped across the black, swung it and started down the shelf trail he had just climbed. He came to the bottom and turned up the creek, following fresh horse tracks he had not noticed in his idle riding. Presently he came around a stony point in the canyon to see his man, who had sat up and was staring toward him.

The fellow wanted none of him and scrambled to his feet, and a gun cracked sharply in the canyon's wild silence. Hack felt the breath of the bullet as it streaked past him, and he whipped the black around and cut hastily into the cover of the jog.

He heard the other horse go clattering up the bed of the creek and wondered about his destination. He retraced his own course to the rim top and from there caught sight of the other rider, who still picked along the creek bottom below, now and then stopping to scan his backtrail.

Insistent curiosity turned Hack off the trail he had followed, and he continued on along the brink of the bluff. He found it easy to keep the wounded man in sight, for the rough going along the canyon bottom had again slowed his horse to a picky walk.

The man was slumped forward in the saddle, now, and swayed so widely he seemed in danger of falling off.

Forward on the slope of a bare mountain, presently, Hack saw the buildings of a small mine with a stockade around it. He rode toward it, cutting a road that looked more used than the trail he had left behind him. He saw the lettering on the side of a building: BIG CASINO MINING CO.

He was about to turn around when the man he had stalked appeared on the canyon top just off from the mine, having used some shelf trail to climb out. Now he rode as if asleep. The horse moved steadily toward the stockade gate, then a man hurried through the gate, previously hidden by the high log fence. He caught the bridle of the horse and led it inside. Hack slipped away.

The road he followed north had been used a lot, and he realized eventually that it came over the hump of War Eagle from Silver. Most of the traffic had been horseback but there was also a scoring of wagon tracks. He topped the mountain soon after nightfall, slipped down through the old camp of Fairview and came into Silver City.

He took the black to the livery, rubbed it

down and ordered it a feed of oats. He had missed yet another meal at the boarding house, so he went into a restaurant and had a late supper. Coming back to the street, he turned down toward the Nolan place, aware of the cool mountain breeze coming up and the million pricks of light in the sky. The excursion into the country had been good for him, for the jaded irritation that had haunted him was gone. He saw a horse standing in front of the boarding house, and as he drew nearer he recognized it as an Oxyoke mount. Jim Corbin was in town again.

He was climbing the stairs to his room when Mary's voice halted and turned him around. She had come into the lower hallway through one of the doors there and was smiling up at him, her shocked aversion of that morning under better control.

"We thought it was you coming in," she said. "Jim and Shelby are in the parlor. They'd like you to join them."

"My pleasure," Hack said and came back down.

Mary took him into the back parlor, a small but pleasant room where she and her mother lived the private family life permissible in a house given over to outsiders. Jim got up from his chair, grinning. Shelby sat on the sofa, her mask only increasing the piquancy of her lovely face. She wore a light summer dress.

"Howdy, Hack," Jim said. "You don't seem to stand still very long."

"Bought a horse and gave him a workout, today. How are you this evening, Miss Shelby?"

"Very well, thank you."

"This gonna be our cattle talk?"

"We hope."

"Sit down," Mary invited, and Hack took a chair.

None of them betrayed any awareness that only yesterday he had killed a man. He supposed it was a shocking thing to the women, and while Jim would understand he was too tactful to allude to it in front of them. Mary left the room, and the others remained quiet through a long moment.

"Well, Hack," Jim said presently, "Shelby tells me you're interested in throwin' in with us."

"More than interested, Jim. As far as I'm concerned it's only a matter of the where-withal. I no longer have the money it takes to talk about a cattle ranch. By next spring, when we can start for Texas for steers, I might have it. I aim to try."

"Now, wait." Jim lifted his hand.

"There's another idea Shelby and me kicked around this evening. We can take over her range in another week. I hate to let it stand idle for the year it would take before we could bring us a herd up from Texas. There's steers to be had closer than that, even if they cost more."

"Like where? The Willamette valley?"

Jim shook his head. "That's easy to drive from, so the price is steep. I'm thinking of the Rogue valley, over west of here. It's isolated. The settlers have a long drive to the railroad and don't often tackle it. They'd be glad to have buyers come in and take delivery on their ranches. We could pick up some pretty good beef steers for fifteen dollars, I think. Cows for ten, with the calves thrown in. Hardly more'n three weeks' drive from there to Shelby's range."

"Using what for money?"

Shelby broke in to say, "I can spare five thousand."

"And I can raise another two," Jim added.

Hack grimaced. "After buying my horse, today, I've got around eight hundred. And I'll need it to eat on till I get hold of what I lost, if I do."

"Let's both eat on it," Jim said quietly. "And put the rest in steers."

82

Hack rubbed his jaw, failing to see where that made him anything but a very minor partner in the enterprise. Unless he got his money back, there was little chance of his being able to put more into it. Their generosity and confidence warmed him, but he didn't aim to freeload. He sat thoughtfully for a moment.

"Are the winters around here always bad?" he asked.

"Well," Jim answered, "it's usually pretty cold from November to April, with plenty of snow mixed in."

"Always snowed in around Christmas?"

"Not always."

Hack leaned forward. "I've been playing with a notion, myself. That horse I bought is in fine shape, and the stableman told me he always ran out on white sage through the winters. That surprised me."

"It keeps 'em fat and sassy. Steers, too."

"Any of it on Shelby's range?"

"Lots of it," Shelby said. "There's an enormous patch of country out there they call the White Sage plateau."

"Runs all the way to Duck Valley," Jim put in. "And in the valley there's the finest summer grass you ever seen. You've got to take a look at it. The two work together. By the time summer grass is gone, the sage starts putting up tendrils that stock likes and that's got plenty of nourishment. That lasts till the grass comes around again. That's why around here you find stock as fat in the dead of a hard winter as in the summer."

"That's what I've got in mind," Hack told them. "If a man could get his beef to the railroad around Christmas, he could get a fancy price. There's hardly any fresh beef coming into the market then."

"He could get through some winters." Jim's eyes reflected his interest. "Others not."

"When he couldn't, he could at least market early in the spring, way ahead of the fall beef shipments, and still get a premium price."

Nodding, Jim started to grin. "That's right. On most ranges they've got to fatten in summer and market in the fall, so that everything's dumped at once. They do that around here, too, just because it's the custom, I reckon."

"You two want to gamble on an untried venture?" Hack asked.

"In a minute," Shelby said.

"Count me in," Jim added.

"All right, let's not buy a mixed herd. Let's get three year steers, only a few hundred head to leave us a little money. We might double the investment by Christmas, at least by April. We might lose everything. But if it works, we could repeat, feeding instead of ranching. It strikes me that's the way to get the most out of the fine winter feed around here."

"It sure is," Jim said with enthusiasm.

"I agree," Shelby said. "It's a good chance to build up our capital fast. And I've got a suggestion, which might make you feel better. Jim and I'll take your I.O.U, for a full third share. You can pay it off when you've collected your money."

"You think I will?"

"I've no doubt of it."

Her quiet confidence uplifted him more than anything that had happened yet. He said, "I take it the range will be back in Shelby's hands by the time we could bring in cattle. How soon could you quit your job, Jim?"

"Right away. The boss knows I'm itching to start up for myself."

Hack could appreciate his eagerness for that. As a cowhand he was in a poor position to be trying to win a wife. "Then do it. When you're ready to leave for the Rogue, I'll be."

"It's a deal."

They all shook hands.

Jim went out to see Mary, which was another important reason for his coming to town. Hack sat watching Shelby, wondering how she would feel if she knew he was positive he had killed the man who threw the lye in her eyes. He was probably the only one who suspected that, and he did not intend to divulge it. She probably would regard it as pure vengeance on his part, as Mary seemed to have done, and Shelby had said specifically that she did not want that.

"I hope you haven't got the wrong idea about the ranch," Shelby said. "There are corrals, a pole barn and a dugout. That's all."

"Good enough. Will you stay on here?"

"Naturally I can't move out with you men."

"Not the way it stands."

Her head lifted. After a moment she said, "Please, Hack. Let's keep this business and friendship."

"Is there a fellow somewhere?"

"No."

"Then I'll make no such an agreement."

She turned her head as if trying to avoid his eyes, and these reactions of a sighted person, still active in her, touched him

86

deeply. He saw that he had made her uncomfortable, so he rose, saying, "Well, if you'll excuse me, I'll hit the hay. I had a long ride."

"Good night."

He went up to his room, realizing with a small sense of shock that he had found the woman he had always wanted, and what had happened to her only endeared her to him. Yet he realized also that the lye had eaten deeper than into the physical areas it had damaged. That was even more outrageous than the blinding. He yearned to find the men behind Murname.

six

Hack walked into the sheriff's office around nine the next morning. Charlie Gilpin was on hand, tilted back in his chair with his feet on the desk and a stogie in his mouth. His eyes widened when he recognized the visitor. He brought his feet down to the floor and stared from under bushy white eyebrows.

"Morning, Sumpter," he said grumpily. "You in trouble again?"

"Not me. But I jumped a wounded man a few miles out of town, yesterday, along toward evening. He whanged a shot at me and lit out."

"Where was this?"

"Close to a mine that calls itself the Big Casino. The thing that puzzles me is that he found what sure looked like a welcome there. Thought I'd see if there'd been a holdup somewhere. Been anything over the telegraph like that?"

Gilpin shook his snowy head. "Nothing's come in to me." His eyes were deeply skeptical. "Hell, man, the Big Casino's Spence Lowell's mine."

Hack stared. "Lowell?"

"Know him?"

"Met him," Hack said. "Just for a minute."

"Well, I've known him for ten years or so," Gilpin returned, "and I can guarantee he ain't harboring renegades. Sounds like you never heard about Spence."

"What's to hear about him?"

"He's a man you got to admire, Sumpter. Ten years ago he was a millionaire, with the mine payin' big. Then come the bust, and he went down like so many others. But there was one way he was plenty different. He never give up. He put every cent he had back into that mine, trying to open a new lead. He kept on even after his money played out, livin' on bacon and beans and doing most of the work himself. Half the country was laughin' at him by then. But he sure showed 'em. He hit pay dirt again, and he's shipping out silver again. Don't tell me a fella like Spence'd traffic with the owlhoot."

Doggedly, Hack said, "But this fellow they took in was wounded. Maybe you know where the South Mountain trail comes up from the crick. I was blowing my horse on top the rim when I seen him down by the crick. He took a bandage off

89

his arm and wet it and put it back on. He was about to fall out of his saddle."

"Lots of ways a man can get hurt. Maybe he got dumped and sprained his arm. Or shot himself accidentally."

"Why'd he take a shot at me when I tried to get down to him?"

"That's wild country," Gilpin said, with an impatient wave of the hand. "How'd he know you weren't trying to rob him?"

"Don't you think you ought to investigate it?"

"I ain't questionin' Spence Lowell about harboring fugitives. Hell, Sumpter, the idea's ridiculous."

"Maybe some of his men are shady."

"Spence wouldn't hire that kind. He's so honest he eventually paid up every cent he owed, even when some of his debts had become outlawed by the statute of limitations. There's been nothin' come in here to indicate your man might be wanted. I reckon you're too anxious to find out what happened to your dinero."

"Not too anxious," Hack snapped. "But anxious enough."

He walked back to the street, disappointed and still puzzled. At first glance he had disliked Lowell, but he did seem to have an amazing record that had inspired a

90

half-reluctant admiration even in him. It seemed stupid to suppose that a man as persistent and scrupulous as he was reputed to be could be tied in with outlaws. Certainly he wasn't going to get the sheriff to concede such a possibility.

Yet he was unable to believe the man he had seen had been hurt accidentally and only feared he would be robbed of his valuables and horse. An innocent man in that condition would welcome help unless he knew he would get it elsewhere very soon. Lowell might have some men on his payroll that were running a sideline without his knowledge. Hack turned down toward the livery stable, deciding to have a closer look at that mine, himself.

Ten minutes later he was riding up the canyon, retracing his course of the previous evening. The summer sun fell hard on the mountain slopes above him, and he could see the collapsing surface works of several of the famous old mines. It came to him that, without the new blood pumped into the country by the thriving and growing cattle industry, Silver City would have ghosted, too. Now it stood fair to survive as a cowtown, even when the last mines were gone, and he hoped to be in and around it all the remaining years of his life.

He topped the mountain presently and began the descent, meeting no one on the road. Not long afterward he sighted the buildings of the Big Casino off across the haze-hung ravine. He followed the dip of the road and made the climb to the open stockade gate. To his surprise a tall, skinny man stepped up promptly to study him with unfriendly eyes.

"Spence Lowell around?" Hack said, puzzled by the man's poorly concealed hostility.

"Maybe and maybe not. Why?"

"I want to see him."

"What about?"

"Supposing I tell him. Where is he?"

The man hesitated, then said, "In the office."

Hack rode on into the mine yard. Up on the tramway a man was pushing an empty ore car back to the mine. He could hear the heavy rumble of the stamp mill down at the foot of the slope. Presently he saw a sign indicating the office, a small, square building needing a coat of paint, and rode toward it. He swung down at the door. It stood open, and he stepped in.

Lowell looked up at him from a desk, and surprise stiffened his cheeks. Then he smiled blandly and got to his feet. "Well, hello, Sumpter. What brings you out this way?"

"Bought me a horse I'm trying out. Seen your mine in the distance and decided to say howdy."

"Glad you did. Sit down."

Hack took the indicated chair and pushed back his hat. "Quite a works you've got here," he commented.

"It's getting back in shape."

"Man was telling me about you. You deserve a medal for stubbornness."

Lowell shrugged. "I knew what I had here. It was just hard to find. I've been hearing about you, too, and the trouble you had with Monk Murname the other day."

"You knew him?"

Lowell laughed. "Hardly. But he hung around Silver the past two or three years, and everybody knew of him. Well, you proved the old rule to him. No matter how good you think you are, a better man comes along. Where'd you learn to handle a gun like that?"

"I did nothing remarkable."

"I heard you drilled him through the heart with one shot."

"He rattled a little worse than I did."

Lowell nodded. "You could say that

about me and my old contemporaries. They panicked and quit. I held on. I just couldn't believe these lodes were all mined out, but they did. I still believe some of the other mines could come back stronger than ever if the capital could be raised. But that's impossible. We don't have the old plunging type of investor, anymore. Everybody wants a sure thing."

"Not everybody," Hack said, remembering the prompt way Jim and Shelby had agreed to gamble on his idea. "You know, I grew up in the old Montana placer country, but I've never been down in a shaft mine. Kind of like to see what it's like down there deeper even than the prairie dogs get."

Lowell's gaze sharpened. "Sorry. This is an old workings, and I haven't been able to keep up repair work. I intend to when I can afford it, but right now it's very dangerous except for experienced men."

It was hard to make up his mind about Lowell. The man had a pleasing personality and an astounding history, yet there were undercurrents at play here that Hack could sense. Grinning, he said, "I wouldn't mind that."

"But I would. I even turned down old Hill, the paper editor, who wanted to do a story on it after I hit pay rock again. I wouldn't take anybody down till the repairs are made, even if they signed waivers releasing me from liability." As if wanting to change the subject, he said, "What're you planning to do with yourself?"

An impulse squirmed into Hack's mind he had not dreamed of a moment before. There might be a way to test this man, if he could set out the bait without betraying his intention.

He said, "I'm still going into the cattle business. Leaving for the Rogue in a few days to pick up a herd."

Lowell straightened, openly staring. "I understood the road agents cleaned you out."

"Not entirely. I had paper money in a belt they never thought to look for. Then I'm taking in a couple of partners — Jim Corbin and Shelby Michaels. We're using her range."

"I know them. Jim's a good man, and I have a world of admiration for Shelby's courage. It was a dreadful thing somebody did to her."

"If I ever find him, I'll kill him."

"The Rogue's a new place to go for steers."

"Too late for another trip to Texas this

year." Hack climbed to his feet. "Well, it was nice seeing you again."

"Drop in any time you're out this way."

Hack walked out into the full sunshine and cast a glance around the yard. In one of these buildings, he was convinced, was a wounded man less than eager to encounter the law. He saw no reason for the skinny guard at the gate and certainly had not liked the man's looks. Lowell's excuse for not showing him the works was plausible, yet the man had been quick and definite with it. Hack dismissed the thought that some of Lowell's employees might be running a sideline. If anyone here was involved in the dirty work, they all were.

He swung into the saddle and rode out through the gate. The skinny man gave him a hard look but said nothing. He was coming out of the ravine and aiming toward War Eagle Mountain when a new slant on the question came to him. Maybe Lowell, about three years ago, had resorted to outlawry as a way to raise money with which to continue developing the mine that had so obsessed his life. His mine seemed to have come in since the trail murders and robberies had started.

Even a tough and tenacious man of honor might be driven to that point after years of poverty-ridden failure and ridicule by those who knew him. The idea furnished a motive, and the man who had had Shelby blinded was obviously an often seen local citizen. He remembered something forgotten until then. Shelby had called one of the men who killed and robbed her father young and good looking.

One thing was certain in a multitude of uncertainties. That was something no one would believe, not even the sheriff, without iron-clad proof. It was something he found difficult to believe, himself.

On top the mountain he came to a turnoff road where crude lettering on a pointing wooden arrow tacked to a tree said: QUEEN BEE. Remembering that as the mine where Dunn Hult was working as a swing shift watchman, he reined in. Dunn should have finished his sleep by now, but he had not mentioned where he was living, and Hack had not run into him around town. They could tell him at the Queen Bee, and it was possible a man like Dunn could make something out of the odd situation at the Big Casino. He turned up the side road.

The mine he soon reached was a replica of Lowell's except that it had no stockade fence. He located the office, swung down

97

and went in. A man wearing an eyeshade and black cuffs swiveled around on his stool at a slanted desk where he was working over a ledger.

"I'm a friend of Dunn Hult's," Hack said. "I want to see him, and I thought maybe you could tell me where he lives."

The man shook his head.

"He works here, doesn't he?" Hack asked.

"Did. But he quit a couple of days ago. Said he aimed to see some country."

Hack stood staring at him. Dunn vanished again? But why? "Well, thanks," he said gruffly.

The man had already turned back to his work.

The surprise of Dunn's cutting out on him again so unexpectedly was nearly as great as that wrought by his sudden suspicions of Spence Lowell. He rode down into Silver and returned his horse to the livery, remembering that he was due to see the doctor again that day. Bethers' dwelling-office was between the livery and Mrs. Nolan's house. Hack turned in and entered an empty waiting room.

Several minutes passed before Bethers emerged. "Lot of good my worrying about you did," he said grumpily, "seeing what you've got yourself into since."

"I didn't hunt for it, Doc."

"That's not the way I heard it. People around here say you're hell on greased wheels."

Hack followed him into the inner room, and the doctor cut off the bandage. "It looks fine," he said. "The sutures can come out, and we can leave off the bandage."

"Good. I can get me a hair cut."

"You do look a little like Wild Bill Hickok."

"Well, I hope you're wrong about me getting his reputation."

"You've got a good start. There's bound to be some cockadoodle along that'll want to try you out."

"Not if I see him coming."

Bethers had snipped the catgut and jerked it out with tweezers. He applied a stinging disinfectant to the newly healed tissue and told Hack he was discharged. Hack paid the bill and went on up the climbing street to Jordan, where he entered a barbershop. A half hour later, his shaggy mane gone, he felt like a presentable man for the first time since he left Texas with the cattle.

A thought came that pleased him, and he

returned to the livery and asked for his black again and also that a good, well-broken horse be saddled with it. He had missed another meal at Mrs. Nolan's, so while waiting for the mounts he crossed the street to a small eating house and had a sandwich and cup of coffee. Then he got the horses and rode down to the boarding house. There was no one in evidence when he entered the house, and he mounted the stairs. Instead of stopping at his own door, he went on to the one at the end of the hallway and rapped.

"Come on," he said when Shelby opened the door. "We're going for a ride."

"Me?" Her mouth dropped open and her head canted back as if she were trying to stare at him.

"Ride, don't you?"

"I used to."

"Then you still do. I've got a horse for you down on the street. It's got a man's saddle. Still own a pair of Levi's?"

"Yes, but —"

"Get into 'em."

He closed the door and stood in the hallway, grinning to himself. She did not mix with the other boarders, and he doubted that she even left the house very often. He heard her moving about beyond the panel, then in a couple of minutes the door opened, and she stood there. Her cheeks were flushed, and she had donned a pair of faded jeans, boots and a shirt, and had caught up her hair in a scarf.

Bowing, he took her hand and placed it on his arm. "Let's get cracking, my lady."

"Where to?"

"I want you to show me our ranch."

"Oh — !" The word choked off. She probably had not been out there since the tragic day she left, and he knew she was both drawn and repelled by his suggestion. "We won't have time, will we?" she faltered.

"We might miss supper."

They descended the stairs. He left her for a moment and found Mary and told her where they were going. Mary looked at him with softening eyes and whispered, "Bless you. Nobody else can get her out of the house, even."

He handed Shelby the reins of the horse she was to ride, and she quickly found the saddlehorn and sprang up. His own doubts fled when he saw the faint smile on her lips. He stepped across the black, saying, "That grey mare's quite a horse," conveying to her what kind of animal she rode, helping her to see it, too. "You'll have to

101

show me how to get out there. Do we go up or down the canyon?"

"The South Mountain trail," she said, "till we're over the mountain. Then east. There isn't much of a road from there on. Just a pair of wheel ruts. It takes us into Black Canyon and down to Axle Creek."

"We'll find it."

They were soon over the mountain, and he recognized the crude Black Canyon road when they reached it and turned, avoiding the need to describe the landmarks and call attention to her handicap. The grey mare followed the black's lead, and Shelby rode very well. The wagon ruts ran ahead of them across the miles of bunchgrass, sage and scabrock. As they traveled, he described the things he noticed, as if she saw them with him.

"That old jack rabbit's going like he had a bee on his behind. Those mountains seem to be floating. The red in those rocks over there is sure bright. That old sun's like a pumpkin in the sky. Wonder how buzzards know when a meal's coming up. Lightning sure raised hob with that old snag."

"Yes," she exclaimed at that point. "I remember it. We're about three miles from home."

"Anybody living there?"

"No, I only leased the range. Oh, it feels so good to be on a horse."

"Funny about that. Sometimes after roundup or a drive, I've swore I never wanted to see a saddle again. After a few days, I'm plain itching to fork one."

"I've missed it," she admitted. "Dreadfully."

"That day's over."

Presently immense swells, footed by black rimrock, began to flank them at a distance, and he knew they were in Black Canyon. "Why'd they call this the Crow Hop plateau?" he asked.

"Indian name. They get some fascinating combinations."

Axle Creek proved to be a stream that came in from a traverse canyon and followed Black on its long journey toward the Snake. A little later he saw a thickened stand of trees by the creek at the foot of a forward knoll, with the vague outlines of a barn showing through the foliage. He said nothing until they had ridden up to it. Corrals ran out from the barn, and the dugout was seated in the footslope of the knob. The setting pleased him.

"Here we are," he said. "It's sure a nice place."

"Isn't it?" she said as if she had forgotten she wasn't seeing it.

She swung down, turning her head about, and he knew she was placing their surroundings in her mind and remembering them. He dismounted and walked to the dugout door, which was not locked. She heard the screak of the rusty hinges and followed him. The interior was dusty, strung with cobwebs, and pack rats had probably moved in. But nothing had been damaged. He knew there were horrible memories attached to it for Shelby, but he did not divert the run of her thoughts.

She stood quietly inside the door, then hesitantly reached out a hand. She moved forward along the wall until her hand touched the rusty stove.

"Hello, there," she said.

Passersby must have eaten a few meals here in the past year, but they had heeded range law and left no mess. The place was comfortably furnished, with curtained bunks along the side and a screened corner where Shelby probably had dressed. It had been provisioned for winter before she had been forced to leave so unexpectedly. There were a lot of canned goods still intact, and while a few sides of bacon were mouldy, the dried beans, rice, flour and coffee were in good containers and still all right. They talked about all that as if she discerned it as much as he, then they went outdoors.

He saw very little that needed repairing, either in the corrals or barn. They climbed a fence and sat on the top rail for a long while, the dropping sun warming their shoulders, while she described the range that ran out from there.

"What time is it?" she said finally.

"We don't have time to reach Silver for supper. Let's rest here before we start."

"You'd have to cook it."

"Nope. I'll start a fire, but you're the cook."

"Me? I can't."

"You know that house, don't you? Where you kept things, the shape and size of them, where everything was located?"

"Yes, but —"

"Let's eat," Hack said.

He walked with her to the door, then went on to the woodpile alone. When he entered the dugout with an armload of split wood, she was seated listlessly in a chair. He brushed the dust from the top of the stove and kindled a fire. She still sat there.

"I'm hungry," he said.

"Where do I start?"

"It's your kitchen and your meal."

He saw her cheeks stain and her body stiffened. She sprang to her feet. "All right, Hack Sumpter. All right."

She began to feel her way about the area given over to cooking purposes. Now and then she took a can down from the shelves, recognizing the contents by the size of the can. She went to the wall where the utensils hung and took down a stew kettle.

"No meat," she said, "and no bread. Would it hurt your manly pride to fill the coffee pot at the spring?"

"Nope."

He went out to the spring house and returned with the granite pot full of water. She had ground up a handful of coffee beans. He put the water on the stove to heat. She took the ground coffee to the stove, approaching it cautiously, gingerly located the pot, lifted the lid and dumped in the coffee. He saw a smile of triumph form on her lips, but she turned away so he could not see it long.

It took time to do the things she had once breezed through. An intimate knowledge of her kitchen helped her, but she had to feel out everything she handled, sometimes puzzling for long moments. She put tomatoes on to stew, finding the can opener and opening the can herself. She opened peaches and punched holes in the condensed milk can, right as to the contents each time, and her triumphant air grew brazen.

"I shouldn't have put the tomatoes on so soon," she said, "because I'm going to bake biscuits. I have a fine oven." She went over, approaching the stove with more confidence as she learned to guide herself by the heat, and slid the stew kettle to the back of the stove.

He smoked a cigarette in patience while she went through the added slow motions, the hard decisions, of getting biscuits batched in a pan.

"I need more water," she said.

He took the teakettle out to the spring and filled it so she could stir up the dough. When he returned she was slicing bacon. "I found a side that doesn't smell too mouldy," she said. "And if it tastes so, you can damned well eat it, anyway. I've got to have grease for the baking pan."

She had been working for an hour when she finally had the meal on the table, but she had accomplished it all herself.

"Now you know," he said when he sat down with her. "You could live here again if you wanted to."

"You and Jim will need the place."

"It could be arranged so that it would be quite proper."

She dropped her fork and seemed to stare at him. "Hack, I told you —"

"But I never agreed."

"You're sorry for me. You don't know me well enough to feel anything else."

"Knew all I needed the first time I talked to you."

"I'll burden no man, least of all you."

"Why me least of all?"

She flushed and did not reply.

He insisted on cleaning up the place, himself, for they would have to hurry to reach Silver by dark. But there was already a new look in Shelby's face, a new confidence.

seven

Five minutes after Hack Sumpter rode out of the mine yard, Spence Lowell stepped out of his office and strode angrily toward the stamp mill. Ed Pointer wasn't there, and Lowell went on up the slope toward the shaft house. He was nearly there when the door opened, and Pointer strode out. Even at the distance, the blocky, neckless man sensed the mood of his boss, and he hurried forward.

"What's eating you, Spence?" he said.

"Sumpter was just here."

"Sumpter? What did he want?"

"To see what he could see. Maybe he was looking for you or Squeaky Anders."

Pointer's eyes narrowed. "He's got no cause to figure I'm here."

"He saw Anders come here. Squeaky said it was a fellow on a black horse, and that's the color of horse Sumpter's riding. Damn Anders. Why'd he have to come here with his troubles?"

"Squeaky?" Pointer returned, himself growing angry. "Because he used to work for you. Figured you'd still stand by him, like you should. And," he added with a trace of contempt, "like you have to."

Lowell swore bitterly. That was one of the weaknesses in his position. He had to traffic with dangerous men and could not protect himself from the ideas they conceived on their own initiative. Anders had been on the dodge for months, then had got into a scrape over a woman and was wounded and he had headed for the Owyhee to recover. Lowell had been sick with his foreboding of trouble from it, but his own men would not let him turn away one of their kind in Anders' plight. He was in their bunkhouse at that moment, being nursed by them, and if Sumpter persuaded the sheriff to come out with a search warrant — Lowell shuddered. But he had worked hard to maintain his reputation, and now maybe the reputation would work for him.

"We've got to do something about Sumpter," Pointer muttered. "It still amazes me the way he handled Monk. It's time Twitch Harper tried his hand."

"No. Not so soon after Monk. I want Twitch to show up in Silver pretending to be a friend of Murname's out to even the score. He hasn't been seen around here, so far as we know, and it would take time for word to reach such a pal of Monk's."

Worriedly, Pointer said, "No telling what Sumpter might do while you're waiting."

"Another possibility's come up, and we might not even need Twitch. Sumpter's going into the Rogue to buy cattle. Obviously he'll carry money."

"You mean —"

"Certainly."

"Where'd you learn that?"

"He told me. I met him at Mary's. He claimed he had just dropped in here sociably. We had a very pleasant chat."

"Oh, sure. In which he baited himself a trap."

"Maybe so, but we'll take the chance. He seems to be closemouthed and does his own doing. If it's a trap, nobody but Corbin would be in on it. We'll have to make sure we get him or both of them."

"Maybe," Pointer said dubiously. "Who do you want to send after 'em?"

"Yarbo and Lacey. They're good at that kind of thing. Meanwhile, have somebody watch Sumpter, so we'll know when he starts for the Rogue."

"I don't much like it."

"Don't you forget," Lowell said hotly. "If a lawman ever comes here with a search warrant, you and I are on our way to the gallows."

Lowell went back to the office and had a drink from his desk bottle. He was shipping enough silver now to defray costs and leave a profit and should have stopped the flow of gold from the cattle trails. But it had been impossible to stop. His men craved money in the same gnawing way he did and, moreover, were conditioned to a life of excitement that made the monotony of what they did in and around the mine particularly galling. It was ironical that if he had been able to stop it even a month ago, he probably would never have had this worry. What was happening at the mine itself caused no alarms and was something no outsider would even remotely suspect.

He sat down in his chair, feeling tired and harried. So Jim Corbin was getting a start in ranching at last. He had never feared the ugly man's competition for Mary as long as he was a low-paid cowhand. But if he made a go of a ranch, which he probably would with Sumpter for a partner, he would be a much stronger threat. So, Lowell decided, they both had to be eliminated on that cattle drive.

Also, he had to demand a decision from Mary before then because he wanted the satisfaction of having her choose him if he could get it.

Lowell prowled his office until six o'clock, then ate in the cookshack with the men. Afterward he singled out Walt Yarbo and said, "Have my trotters hitched up. I'm using the caleche, tonight." He went to his private quarters and drew a bath, the tub and hot water being luxuries remaining from the days when he had been a rich man, and he lay in the water a long while trying to soak the tensions out of his body. He had borne his adversity too long for his own good, he thought. He should have found the way out much sooner.

He stood naked by the mirror and shaved carefully, approving of his good shoulders and the proud set of his head. He disdained cologne afterward but used a tan talcum to take the aftershave shine from his face. He combed his hair and dressed in his best shirt and suit. He wanted everything in his favor that night.

The rubber tired caleche, which rode like a cloud, was tied in front of the building when he stepped out into the waning day. He sprang to the seat, took the reins and drove out of the stockade. The skinny Yarbo shut the gate behind him. Unless opened especially, it would stay padlocked from then until daylight.

He drew up in front of the Nolan house a little after seven-thirty and tied the team to the ring at the edge of the sidewalk. He had forced the last look of worry from his face and appeared jaunty as he swung up the path, mounted the steps and knocked. Mary answered and showed her pleasure at seeing him.

"Good evening, Spence. My, you're dressed up tonight."

"A man needs reminding that he's something more than a gopher."

"Come in."

"There's light enough left for a spin. How about it?"

"I'd love it. I've been feeling cooped up, this afternoon. Hack and Shelby rode out to her ranch."

"Shelby?" he said in surprise.

She laughed gayly. "Hack seems able to boss her. You know after that business with Monk Murname, I thought he was a brutal man. I was wrong. He has a surprising tenderness."

"Well, don't fall for him." Lowell pretended to tease, but his eyes were cold.

"I won't. But I think Shelby could if she'd let herself."

"Why won't she?"

"She's convinced she'd only be a drag on a man."

They went down the path and got into the sleek buggy. Lowell took the reins and followed Washington to Jordan, then turned down the canyon, the matched trotters spanking along and the vehicle moving lightly, soundlessly. He saw Mary lean back in the seat, enjoying it. She had never looked so lovely, and he had never wanted her so achingly.

"You know, Mary," he said quietly, "I've waited since you were ten years old for you to grow up."

She turned quickly to look at him. "Do you expect me to believe that?"

"It's true. There was something about you even as a little girl that won my heart, back when I was poor and your mother's boarder, myself. I've never looked at another woman."

"Are you really serious? You must have known you were soon considered the catch of the camp. And there were plenty of desirable women here, too."

"I know that. And I couldn't see them. Later, when everything went wrong, I worked to save the mine for you. You know I'm not given to flattery, Mary. I mean what I say."

"I — I'm touched, Spence. I've known that you've been interested in me in recent years but —"

"I never told you before," he said, "because I wanted to tell you when I asked you to be my wife. Will you?"

He saw her breath catch, and she looked forward at the horses. His hopes fled. Then she looked back at him, her face grave. "Is it all right if I say I can't answer that yet? I just don't know, Spence. I've grown awfully fond of you. I admire you tremendously."

"Is it Corbin? Are you in love with him?"

She made a helpless motion with her hands. "It's the same thing there. I like Jim enormously, but no more than I like you. Spence, I just can't say right now. I don't seem to be in love. At least, not yet."

"That will come," he said pleadingly. "In another few years I'll have a fortune. We can leave the Owyhee. I plan a very fine home for us in San Francisco. I'd like to travel, to see Europe and maybe the rest of the world. But I want none of it unless you share it with me."

"That's pretty heady stuff for a girl," Mary said softly. "I won't say things like that don't attract me. They do any honest person. But I wouldn't want to marry a man, even one I liked a lot, for them. Wait a while longer, Spence — will you?"

"Mary, I've waited so long." He wanted to grab and crush her in his arms, to render her helpless with feelings that must lie in her heart. But she was a gentle, sheltered girl. He dared not risk offending her. He sighed. "But I've also learned how to be patient. I can wait longer, but don't make it too long. Please. I must have your answer soon."

"All right, Spence."

They talked no more about it, driving on to Booneville and coming back up the canyon in the deepening evening.

Mary came out of her thoughts when Lowell pulled up in front of her house, saying with an attempt at lightness, "I baked a chocolate cake, this afternoon. You have time to come in, don't you?"

"With pleasure," he replied.

Presently, when he was in the back parlor waiting for her to make coffee, he realized that he was developing a headache. Frustration had always been intolerable to him, and he had gained nothing that he had not already possessed, only a reaffirmation of his eligibility. The little nerve needles began to prick him, and his resentment of his rival and the man who had got him in another tight corner mounted with each breath he drew. Yet he managed to smooth all that from his countenance when Mary came back with cake and coffee.

At that moment footsteps sounded in the hallway, and Shelby's voice called, "Hello. We're back."

"Come on in," Mary answered.

Lowell swore silently when Sumpter appeared in the doorway behind the blind girl. They had seen the buggy in front and were not surprised to find him here, and Sumpter's face was relaxed, his manner pleasant. Lowell avoided looking at Shelby for he was always deeply uneasy in her presence.

"Evening, Lowell," the puncher said blandly. "Nice team you've got out front."

"Yes."

Shelby turned in the direction of his voice and smiled at Lowell, saying, "Good evening, Spence." There was a healthy glow in her cheeks and a dusting of tan from her ride in the sun. He had never seen her look so happy, so normal, and remembered what Mary had said about her and Sumpter. Well, she would never be put through the need of a decision about marrying the man. She was not going to get the chance. If there was ever a possibility of his reconsidering his intentions toward Sumpter, it was destroyed in that moment.

"Evening, Shelby," he answered. "Mary tells me you went out to the ranch."

She nodded. "We ate out there."

"Room for some cake and coffee?"

"Always," Hack said for them.

The girls went into the kitchen. Sumpter sat down, a barbarian by Lowell's standards but oddly poised and confident.

"How's the black working out?" Lowell said.

"Fine. He's a good horse."

"Taking him to the Rogue, I suppose."

"He's taking me. Jim Corbin's bringing a little cavvy from Oxyoke, but the black boy's my top horse."

"Corbin's going with you?"

Sumpter nodded.

"Will you be able to hire a trail crew in that country? I understand they're mostly farmers, over there."

The puncher grinned. "Won't need much of one. We only aim to pick up a few hundred head of threes to fatten for market. We can handle 'em ourselves after they're trail broke. Might hire a man to help the first few days."

Lowell sipped his coffee, dropping his

gaze. That meant they wouldn't have as much gold along as he had supposed. But horses alone were attractive enough to some of the ruthless rascals that ran in the back country, and reason enough for them to be attacked.

The women came back with refreshments for Shelby and Sumpter, and Lowell fancied that there was something especially appreciative in the way Mary glanced at Sumpter now and then. The icy thought slid into his mind: What if he's the one she finds she can fall in love with? Lowell's hands were trembling, so he put down the cake plate and cup and rose to his feet.

He said, "Thanks for a pleasant evening, Mary, but I've got to go. My work's a little heavy right now." He exchanged good nights with the other two and left the room. Mary followed him.

At the door she said quietly, "I hope I haven't offended you, Spence."

"Of course not." He managed to sound as if he meant it. He drove up to Jordan Street and turned toward the head of the canyon, haunted by memories of when he had been in the flush of youth himself, ambition burning like a hot coal in his brain and his heart swollen with the courage with which to fulfill it. He remembered the delight of finding luck was on his side when he made the off-chance discovery of the Big Casino's one good ore body, and the pride of being accepted by other men of success as one of them, all above the common run simply because they were successful. Yet he had not known when he was well off.

He had not blandished Mary with his account of the long years he had waited for her. At first he had thought his preoccupation with a girl not even nubile to be abnormal and it had worried him. Yet there had been no lust in it, no thought of doing her harm. He had simply been drawn to her powerfully, delighting in her raven hair, her lively brown eyes, her sweet girlish ways, her vague promise of lush womanhood. It must have robbed him of interest in the women on hand at that time, and he hadn't even indulged in the purely carnal pleasures available to a man in his position. All his drives and all his dreams were concentrated, like sun through a magnifying glass, on Mary and his mine.

Lowell came out of his thoughts to realize that he was running down the south slope of War Eagle. He felt the breeze of the open plateau and looked up to see a blazing skyful of stars. The horses paced on at their mile-eating clip and had traveled this road too often to need attention. He thought of giving them to Mary to help his chances of winning her, but they would be too expensive for her to maintain.

He came up to the closed stockade gate in about half an hour and shouted. Presently the gate swung open, and he drove in. Several of the men had come out of the nearby bunkhouse, surprised by his early return and worried that something was wrong. He turned the rig over to them, refusing to satisfy their curiosity, and strode on toward his own living quarters.

He took off his coat and shoestring tie and sat down with a drink, remembering the night when he had made the decision from which there was no turning back. It had been in the cattle shipping season, and he knew that fortunes in gold were moving on the various lonely trails just then. He had knocked off the first one himself and got money with which to continue exploring in the mine.

It had produced nothing but tons of barren rock and finally he had admitted that there was no fortune provided by Nature waiting for him down in the drifts. Slowly the other plan shaped itself in his mind, for which he needed men of the right disposition. Gradually he had gathered them, including a number that were not around anymore, and the backtrails had continued to pay the overhead while he went after his bonanza in another way.

Only once, before Sumpter showed up, had he been thrown into a state of nerves like this. Since his men were all too eager for the excitement of the backcountry work, he had been quite willing to leave it to them. Then one day Ed Pointer, who had been in Winnemucca, hurried in with word that a Black Canyon rancher was nearing there with the proceeds from a herd.

They had long since decided that the strikes were faster and safer with two men, and there had been no one available just then to send with Pointer. He had declined to accompany Pointer, preferring to pass up the chance, until the man hinted at cowardice. Realizing that he could not control men like this if he lost their respect, he had been forced to go along. They had retrieved the situation after it became badly fouled, but he still paid for it every time he saw Shelby Michaels. And he had proved his nerve, which satisfied the men so that he had not been forced to go out again.

eight

The saddle horses were waiting on the street. Hack said goodbye to the Nolans and left Jim Corbin talking with Mary while he climbed the stairs and knocked on Shelby's door. He would be gone at least six weeks, depending on their luck in getting the steers they wanted in the Rogue, and he would miss the dark, slender girl who had changed all his concepts of the future. She seemed to have expected him, for the door opened quickly.

"Well, so long," he said.

"Good luck, Hack." She held out her hand.

"I'd like to ask a favor."

"If there's anything I can do, I'd be glad to."

"Go around town with Mary. Don't dodge the other boarders."

"That's a favor?"

"Yes."

"All right."

"Promise?"

"Yes."

"Then *adios*."

"*Hasta luego,* Hack."

He was soon riding down the canyon with Jim in the bright August morning. There was hardly a breath of wind, and the mounting warmth of the earth rendered up its strong mineral smells. All along the canyon, the creek below the road showed the blanched tailings left by early placer miners, and the slopes above were pitted by the countless prospects that had probed War Eagle. Now and then they passed the caving ruins of old stamp mills, and the ghostly remains of Ruby City fell behind.

Well below Wagontown the stage road left the creek for a time, and the riders followed the road to enter country Hack had not seen before, the west slope of the plateau that dropped from the mountains to the great desert of the Owyhee river. They passed stage stations and a few times saw ranch buildings off in the haze blued distance, and cattle began to show their dotted shapes among the upthrusts of red lava.

They nooned from their saddlebags and in early afternoon stopped off at a ranch where Jim had left the extra horses and a camp outfit he had brought over from Oxyoke, which lay to the north. They were back on Jordan Creek by then and moved swiftly down its valley, the desert spreading below them like a sheet of crumpled, dusty zinc. They crossed the river in late afternoon, thereafter following up the canyon of Crooked Creek toward the distant Pueblos on the Nevada line. Around six they made camp in the canyon.

While they were eating supper, Hack said, "Jim, we're bait for the bunch that lifted my dinero."

"That's to be expected."

"More than a little, this trip. I flavored the bait with one man in particular. I've got a hunch he took it."

"What man?"

"If I told you, you'd call me crazy. Let's see what happens."

They hobbled the horses on the grass and made up their beds by the campfire, afterward smoking and talking over their prospects while night came on. The wildness of their environs pleased Hack, and he wished he could describe it to Shelby. Coyotes had chosen to serenade the fire from the far rim of the canyon. Hot desert scents still came to them on the gentle breeze. There was a crystalline depth to the star blazing sky. He wondered why men complicated their needs the way they did when some of the deepest satisfactions lay in simple things easy to experience.

Yawning presently, Jim said, "Think we should take turns sleepin' tonight?"

"For a few nights, anyway," Hack answered. "If my man don't take bait, others seen us in the bank getting the money."

He tossed the stub of his cigarette into the fire, looking about. He had picked the site carefully because he wanted to make this camp invite attack to relieve, if possible, the strain of waiting for it to happen. The other night, in the Nolans' back parlor, he had sensed the seething hostility in Spence Lowell. He had marked the probing questions that the man asked him about his plans.

They were close to the north rim of the canyon, which had begun to pinch in at its head, and cottonwood along the creek screened the roundabout flat. The trail was on the far side of the creek, and they had left the stake road that afternoon and taken a less travelled route into California and western Oregon. They were seventy miles from Silver City, much farther than he had been when he was bushwhacked on the Bruneau.

Hack said, "We might be being watched, so we better turn in till the fire dies down." They placed their saddles at the head of the beds for pillows, pulled off their boots and bedded down.

An hour later the fire had dwindled to coals. Hack called to Jim and found him awake. They slipped out of their blankets and went over to the packs and got a couple of tarps and rolled them. Then they arranged the rolls in their places in the deserted beds. Leaving their hats still on the saddles and their boots by the side of the beds, they moved off into the trees, wearing their guns and carrying saddle blankets.

"Might as well catch some sleep," Hack said, tossing Jim his blanket. "I'll call you to spell me in a couple of hours."

Jim stretched out at the base of a cottonwood and covered himself. Hack sat down nearby, pretty well concealed from the camp but able to see it in the starlight. The illusion of a normally sleeping camp was convincing. But if the trail wolves distrusted it, there would be wearing days of expecting trouble momentarily.

He waited an interminable while, growing cold as the ground lost its head and the air grew chilled. He was moving over to rouse Jim for his watch when the crack of a rifle shot split the wild silence of the night. It came from the nearer rim, and a succession of shots beat out. Hack saw the hats knocked off their perches, and the blankets jumped as heavy lead slugged into them, proving that the gunman was an excellent shot. The onslaught stopped and was followed by a complete silence.

Jim raised up, and Hack whispered, "Keep quiet. They'll be in for the money, and they'll come in jumpy."

He could hear Jim's heavy breathing, and blood was thumping in his own lungs and head. It had worked so far, but there was ticklish business ahead.

The wait seemed longer than the one before. The attackers were on the rim and had to get down, but they had had time for that. The lack of retaliation from the camp could not have frightened them away, for no one could have lived through the fusillade that had riddled the beds. Hack felt his muscles ache from the enforced immobility, then Jim's hand touched his leg. At the same time Hack saw shadows from under a tree beyond the camp.

They came out slowly, a tall man and a fat one. The skinny one carried a rifle and the other had a pistol gripped warily in his hand. They placed each step with care, intently staring at the beds. The fire had died now to only an occasional wind fanned glow, but there was enough starlight to let Hack see. The tall man was the guard he had seen on the gate at the Big Casino. He did not place the fat one. They reached the camp, and the tall one kicked the closest bed and abruptly split the night with a yell.

"Hell, Frank — it's a fake! Get outta here!"

"Hold it!" Hack shouted.

They wheeled toward him and started shooting.

Jim was up with his rifle, and it whacked its sound into the bedlam. The two men were backing toward the trees they had emerged from. Hack placed his first shot with care, and the fat man threw up his arms, turned dizzily about and fell. The other broke and raced into the cover of the cottonwoods, dodging the bullets that sought him. Hack bolted after him, impeded by his tender bare feet. The tall man went crashing through the underbrush, then the sound stopped. Hack slowed, shifted his course, and went on with caution. In a moment he heard the thunder of hoofs on the far side of the trees.

"Well, we got one," Jim breathed, when Hack returned to the camp. "I know 'em. Walt Yarbo and Frank Lacey. They work at the Big Casino."

"Which is this?"

"Lacey. He's dead." Jim's voice conveyed his shock. "What do you make of it? They worked at that mine a long while."

"I make plenty of it, Jim. The man I told about this cattle deal was Spence Lowell."

"Hell, he couldn't be in on a thing like this."

"Couldn't he? How'd these two know about it if he didn't tell 'em?"

"I can't believe it, Hack. Not Lowell."

"He's the man back of the whole rotten business." Hack looked around. "Well, Yarbo was plenty boogered and won't give us any more trouble right off. So we might as well freshen the fire and warm up."

Hack threw more wood on the coals. They carried the body over under a tree and put a tarp over it, then returned to the fire. Jim sat down, shaking his head and rubbing his eyes.

"Lowell's got to be the man," he admitted presently. "And what if Mary's in love with him?"

"We can't help that, Jim. Lowell's taking money off the trails to run his mine and keep his renegade outfit happy. Half a dozen men have been murdered, maybe more that weren't reported. He's responsible for Shelby's blindness. Everyone that knows his story thinks he's an admirable

131

character, but he's as low as they come."

"What'll we do?"

"Turn back and take Lacey's body to the sheriff. Yarbo'll head back to the mine. If we can get Gilpin to act quick enough, he might catch him there. He could find a wounded renegade I seen go under cover there, too. I told Gilpin about him, but he wasn't persuaded."

"I'll be damned." Jim's lingering incredulity indicated the difficulty of rooting Lowell out from behind the reputation he had made for himself by his overt actions. "That's the way some of them mining people get. When they think they've got a bonanza waiting for 'em, they'll do almost anything to get to it."

"Maybe he hasn't even got a bonanza."

"He's shipping bullion."

"Maybe he's melting down the gold and selling it to the mint as new mined."

Jim shook his head. "That's a silver mine. He couldn't keep the mint from getting suspicious unless he shipped silver. So he must be getting it out of his mine."

"Maybe he's stolen bullion shipments from other mines, too, and ships it as his own product."

"Hasn't been word of that kind of thing for a long while. The stages and express cars're guarded too good, nowdays, and mines guard what they've got on hand."

Hack's doubts still nagged him. "I hear he hunted for his bonanza seven years. It doesn't make sense that, even if there was a genuine one in the Big Casino, it would take that long to find it."

They slept the remaining hours of the night, and roused at daybreak, made breakfast and packed the camp. With Lacey's body wrapped in a tarp and lashed to his horse, which they found nearby, they started back toward Silver City. Around noon they dropped the cavvy at a stage station on the Nevada road, agreeing to pay board until they got back, and thus lightened hurried on up the hot plateau. Though they crowded their horses to the limit, they did not reach Silver until the edge of darkness had slid in on the town.

They pulled up in front of the courthouse, and Hack left Jim with the horses while he went into the building. The sheriff's office was locked. He went down to the jail office and found Bales, the town marshal, on hand.

"Where's Gilpin?" Hack asked.

"Went home. What's up?"

"I'll tell him. Where does he live?"

"Up on the hill."

"I don't know that section. Send somebody after him, Bales. I got a dead man outside."

"Bring him in," Bales returned. "I reckon he'll keep till morning."

"Damn it, Bales, it's urgent. Gilpin's got to do something tonight, or it'll be too late."

"All right, I'll send for him."

Hack waited impatiently with Jim for what seemed half an hour. Finally Charlie Gilpin came along the walk and stopped to stare at the limp wrapped shape lashed to the third horse. "Who is it?" he said gruffly.

"You knew Frank Lacey, out at the Big Casino?"

"Yeah."

"It's him. He and Walt Yarbo shot up our camp, last night. We expected it and left dummies and were waiting for 'em. Yarbo got away, and he's back at the mine by now, if Lowell hasn't sent him packing again. You've got to get out there, Sheriff, right now. If you want help, swear in me and Jim as deputies."

Gilpin held up his hand. "Now, wait a minute. That's twice you've accused Spence Lowell of workin' with the owl hoot. I ain't even seen who you've got under that tarp."

Sighing, Hack said, "Okay, let's pack him inside."

When the body had been carried into the courthouse and identified by the sheriff, the officer was still dubious. "You don't know that the other man was Yarbo or where he went."

"Do you want a tintype picture of him?"

Gilpin bristled. "To walk in on Spence Lowell with arrest warrants, I want to know what I'm doing."

"You don't have time to get warrants. We've got to get out there pronto."

"Not without warrants. Not on your wild guesses."

Desperately, Hack said, "By tomorrow Yarbo'll be on his way to yonder. So'll the wounded renegade I saw go in there, that you'd ought to have picked up a week back."

"We'll see the circuit judge in the morning, but I doubt he'll issue warrants on nothing but your say-so. You've got a complaint against Lacey that'll clear you at the inquest. You're just stringing the rest of it together."

"All right," Hack said wearily, and he and Jim went back to the street. The trap and its risks had proved his suspicions and opened the eyes of only one other person

— Jim. He knew already that nothing more than that would come of it.

"I don't want to put up at the boarding house," Jim said. "Mary would want to know what brought us back, and we'd have to tell her. Let's take a hotel room."

"Suits me better, too," Hack agreed. He had given up his room there since he would be going to the ranch when they got back from the drive, although Mrs. Nolan put up transients when she had the room.

nine

When Yarbo rode past the office windows alone, Lowell knew from his disturbed countenance that something was seriously wrong. He had waited all morning for their return, confident that it would mark the end of the danger that had threatened him ever since Hack Sumpter survived the Bruneau ambush. He started to rise from his chair, then settled back in a sudden feeling of weakness, waiting for Yarbo to come in. The door pushed inward, and the thin man walked through, his eyes increasing Lowell's uneasiness. At the same time Ed Pointer's figure strode past the windows, and Pointer followed in on Yarbo's heels.

"What's wrong, Walt?" Pointer said as he entered. He had noticed the man riding through the mine yard and derived the same disturbing reaction Lowell felt.

"Well," Yarbo said weakly, "they got Frank."

"You mean Sumpter and Corbin?" Lowell exclaimed, shoving to his feet. "They're still alive?"

"Without a scratch," Yarbo said in a hangdog voice. "They took us like Grant took Richmond. Kee-rist!"

Pointer flung Lowell a hard stare. "I told you it was a trap, but you had to be shown!"

Anger oozed through the shock in Lowell, and it was in the eyes that raked Yarbo mercilessly. "You stupid bums. Is Lacey dead?"

"Dunno. But they've either got him or his carcass. They'll take it to the law sure. They couldn't help but recognize me. I've got to light out of this country."

Lowell drew the whiskey bottle from his desk and handed it to Yarbo. "Take a pull on that, then tell us what happened."

Yarbo tipped the bottle to his lips and seemed thirsty enough to empty it. Pointer removed it from his hands, and the thin man shuddered. He wiped his mouth with the back of his hand, fear haunting his deep-set eyes.

"It was a pretty setup," he said defensively, and went on to tell what had happened on Crooked Creek. "I got the hell outta there," he concluded, "and that's the size of it. I'd have kept goin' except I wanted to warn you. Gilpin'll be out here after me, sure, and you've got to be ready for him."

"Yeah," Pointer said worriedly, "and we've got Squeaky Anders on our hands. He'll have to light out with you."

"All right," Lowell said, glowering at Yarbo. "You asked for it, Walt. Pick up Anders and get traveling."

"Not," Yarbo said, "without some dinero, and quite a bit of it."

"You always got your cuts at the time you had them coming."

"Chicken feed. If I don't knock a hole in the skyline, you won't ever get your bonanza outta the mine. You'll swing, too. I figure that's worth plenty to you, Spence. It ain't fun bein' on the dodge. I reckon you can afford to make it worth my while."

"Damn you. How much?"

"Ten thousand might hurry me a little."

"Preposterous."

"Then I'm in no rush at all."

A chill trembled through Lowell's body. If Sumpter and Corbin had left the camp immediately, they could reach Silver as speedily as Yarbo had. The prisoner or body would be enough to persuade the sheriff to come out here. Yarbo's usefulness was over, and he had become a bright new danger, himself. Lowell rose and walked over to the big iron safe that stood in the corner of the office. He hunkered while he worked the combination and swung open the door. There were buckskin bags of gold coin in there, and something else he had put there long ago in case one of his men ever forced him to open this door.

His hand darted in and grabbed the gun. He swiveled on the balls of his feet and pointed the piece on an upslant at Yarbo, savoring the shock on the man's face. He fired a shot into the man's belly, another into the center of his chest. Yarbo came down in a curling drop.

Pointer stood aghast. "Christ, Spence!"

"You heard him blackmail me," Lowell said coldly. "Do you think one payoff would have satisfied him? If he found he could do it, he'd be back after me, time and again."

"Yeah," Pointer said on an expulsion of breath. "I guess that's right."

"Weight and dump him into the sump of that old air shaft. Anders is in no shape to ride by himself. Get rid of him the same way."

"Now, look here —"

"Charlie Gilpin's apt to ride through the gate any minute. He might have a warrant to search us from end to end. There's no hiding Anders safely and no time for you to get him away from here. Do what I said."

"Okay." Pointer's face was white when he walked to the door and yelled. A man came hurrying over from the nearby stable. The new arrival recoiled when he saw the body, but Pointer said tersely, "He tried to doublecross us. Help me get him to the shaft house."

Yarbo had not bled badly in the short time he had lain there, and Lowell mopped up the dribble and used more water to remove the last stains from the floor. He washed his hands, examined his clothing for telltale marks, then locked the safe door. The room smelled of powder smoke, so he opened the door and windows to let the breeze fan it out. He took another drink and sat down at the desk, feeling weak and ill.

He watched the windows, expecting momentarily to see riders appear out there from Silver City. Presently the room smelled fresh, and the wet stains on the floor had dried. He closed all but one window, stopping the heavy breeze. An hour passed with nothing happening, then Pointer came back in. He looked surly, not liking what he had been forced to accept.

"So what was the big sweat about?" he

said. "I ain't seen any sheriff."

"We couldn't be sure," Lowell answered. "Is everything taken care of?"

"It's done. And I suppose that's what I can expect before the big payoff."

Stung by the contempt in his foreman's eyes, Lowell snapped, "What do you propose to do about it? You couldn't make yourself a nickel without me and this mine. You're not in a position to get high and mighty."

Pointer grimaced. "We're gonna be handicapped with Frank and Walt gone. Twitch Harper can't work in the open. There's nobody else I'd trust out of my sight."

Lowell had been thinking about that. Pointer, Yarbo and Lacey had been running mates at the time he took them on, and that, rather than moral compunction, accounted for Pointer's hostility. They had been the only ones who knew as much about his activity as he did. The half dozen others working around the mine and taking care of the horses were of the same stripe, but were well paid to do what they were told and to keep their mouths shut. That was all that contingent expected to get out of it.

"We'll worry about it after we see what happens," he said.

Pointer stumped out.

The afternoon wore away, and the sheriff did not put in an appearance. Instead of relieving Lowell, it only increased his apprehension. Something big was transpiring, he decided, the legal business of getting search and arrest warrants signed by the judge.

It was after ten the next morning when Gilpin pulled up in front of the office and swung out of the saddle. He looked uneasy but had come out alone. Lowell pretended to be writing a letter and looked up, smiling in surprise.

"Why hello, Charlie," he said cheerfully. "What brings you out this way?" He nodded toward a chair by the window, and Gilpin walked to it and sat down heavily. "Chasing somebody?"

"It's about a couple of your men, Yarbo and Lacey. They around, this morning?"

"I wouldn't know, Charlie. Ed Pointer handles the crew. I seldom know what goes on with them."

"What do you know about that particular pair?"

Lowell wrinkled his brow. "Well, they've worked here quite a while. They're both boozers and like to cut loose. But I don't allow that here, so they go off on tears now and then. It makes Ed sore, but they're good men and when they come back repentant he takes 'em back."

"One won't ever come back again," Gilpin said. "Frank Lacey's down in the morgue. Him and Yarbo tried to take some money off Sumpter and Corbin, out on the Crooked, the other night. They brought Lacey's body in last night. Yarbo got away."

"What's that?" Lowell got just the right shock into the question.

"It's a fact," Gilpin said grimly. "Them two were tryin' to make a raise, maybe to finance their good time."

"I'll be damned. I suppose you've got a warrant for Yarbo."

Gilpin nodded. "Spence, this goes against my grain, but there's somethin' I've got to take up with you. Sumpter claims you were back of them two and the other trail bushwhacks. Says you're the only one he told about goin' to the Rogue for steers that could have tipped off the pair that hit him."

"You mean to say you believe that?" Lowell said with rounded eyes.

"For a fact, I can't, Spence. But the charge was made and I couldn't ignore it. You did know they were going for steers and would naturally be carrying money?"

144

"Sure. We talked about it here, then again at the Nolan house. Several people must have known about it. Why single me out?"

"He says you've financed your explorations that way."

"He says! And I suppose that's all it takes to convict me."

"Hold your horses, Spence." Gilpin lifted a placating hand. "It just don't make sense a man with the stuff you've showed would resort to that. I allow there's other ways Yarbo and Lacey could have learned about it. If they were boozers and high livers, they just wanted some good time money."

Lowell was growing enheartened, and he took a chance. "If you think I'm hiding Yarbo here, look around. And you won't even need a search warrant." He scarcely dared to breathe for, if Gilpin took him up and went through the works, it would imply less faith than he claimed he possessed. And worse. He was not a mining man, but he might notice things to increase any suspicions Sumpter might have planted.

Gilpin shook his head. "Your word's good enough. Yarbo's miles from here by now. I'll get on the telegraph."

"You think Sumpter's making his talk in public?"

"Doubt it. He's close mouthed."

"I don't know what he's got against me. I hardly know the man."

"He lost a lot of money. I reckon he's inclined to see suspects behind every clump of sage. Don't worry about me spreadin' it, either. I won't." Gilpin rose from his chair. "I hope you realize I had to question you about it."

"Sure. And I appreciate your confidence."

Lowell was smiling when Gilpin rode off. His reputation had stood him in better stead than he had dared to hope. He congratulated himself on the poise with which he had handled the situation. Hack Sumpter was no longer a menace to him. Nothing he could say would be believed where it counted, and he had been as close as he would ever come to a shred of proof.

Pointer came in to see what had taken place. "It's all right," Lowell assured him. "From here on we're taking no chances. We've got enough without that."

"How about Sumpter?"

"He's powerless. He didn't rouse Gilpin enough even to make a search."

"Now, wait a minute," Pointer protested.

146

"Sumpter's not going to rest till he's pinned something on us. Not if it takes him months. You were lucky this time, and maybe it made you too sure of yourself again. We've got to send Twitch after him."

Lowell considered a moment. "All right. No outsider has ever seen Twitch here. Send him off tonight. He's to go down into Nevada and drift back to Silver over the stage road. I'm taking no chances on his being tied to us in any way."

"Okay. So let's set somethin' straight between you and me private. Don't get the notion of dealin' me out sudden, someday, so you won't have to share with anybody at all or have someone around who might blackmail you. Don't ever start thinking along that line about me, Spence." Pointer walked out.

ten

After a day in the Rogue valley, Hack knew they had come to the right place. The country teemed with cattle, which the isolated settlers were glad to get off their hands so easily. It was a breed built up from cattle brought across the plains by wagon emigrants, compact and weighty, and mixed with hardy Spanish cattle from California. Within a week he and Jim had bought four hundred head at the hoped for price. They hired a settler to help brand and accompany them for a few days while the cattle settled to the drive.

Seven weeks after their delayed departure from Silver City they were back within easy riding distance. When they had finished their supper, Hack grinned at Jim and said, "I can handle the herd tonight, and you're itching to see Mary. Go on in."

Jim laughed. "I bet you're as itchy to see Shelby."

"Match you."

Jim pulled out a coin and flipped it. Hack called heads and, somewhat to his embarrassment, won the toss.

"No backin' out," Jim said. "We won't be so far away but I can do my own wooing tomorrow night."

Hack went down to the creek on which they had stopped for water for the cattle, took a bath and shaved, then donned the last change of clothes in his war bag. The days were shortening as the autumn equinox drew nearer, and he rode into Silver in the last fading light.

To his disappointment, Spence Lowell's sleek buggy was tied in front of the Nolan house. He did not trust himself to encounter the man now, and rode back onto Jordan Street, racking his horse in front of the Pay Dirt. He stepped into the saloon to find it fairly crowded, since it drew a lot of floaters from the street's two hotels. Most of the patrons wore business clothes, although a few were dressed for riding, like himself. He stepped up to the bar.

It surprised him that the bartender recognized him immediately, since he had only been in here a few times. "Howdy, Sumpter," the apron said heartily. "We ain't been seein' you around."

Hack remembered how that big room at the courthouse had overflowed from the crowd of sensation seekers who had attended the inquests on Murname and Lacey, both men who had died by his gun. This was evidence of the notoriety it had brought him, and he felt a riffling aversion to it.

"That's right," he agreed. His tone discouraged further conversation, and he ordered a whiskey.

"So you're Sumpter," a voice said at his side.

Hack turned his head, for the first time really noticing the little man who stood there. He was young, wore a grin, and his bandy legs were encased in California pants. A gun rode his hip, and Hack's eyes narrowed. The weapon had notches filed on the handle, several of them, so conspicuous they had to be noticed. That seemed to be what the wearer wanted.

"That's what they call me," he said.

"Heard about you." The grin left the bantam's face and came back. "You gonna be around a while?"

"Did I ask your intentions?"

A thin shoulder twitched. The man laughed. "I wouldn't be touchy about it if you had, Sumpter. I'll tell you without askin'. I aim to be around a while. See you, maybe." He tossed a coin on the bar and, with a little man's cocky stride, went swinging out through the doorway.

Hack looked at the bartender. "Where'd that blow in from?"

"Got me, but he's been here a week or so. They call him Twitch Harper. Talks like he's been down in them tough mining camps in the south end of Nevada."

"Figurin' to file himself another notch here?"

"Wouldn't doubt it. Acts like a fightin' cock out for trouble. We get 'em here, as you ought to know. Cusses like Monk Murname." The apron pushed back the coin Hack had dropped. "On the house, Sumpter. It's a pleasure to see the genuine article after that counterfeit."

"What do you mean?"

"You didn't know why he give you that insolence?"

"Why did he?"

"He'd heard about you. Remember? You better keep an eye on the little varmint. He figures if he can lift your scalp, he'll be a big man in these parts. Cusses like him take to that like a horse to loco weed."

Hack refused to regard it seriously. He had left his gun in camp and was glad of it. If the grinning, glory hunting kid tried to give him trouble, he would step around it and go back to the herd.

He rode down to Washington Street and saw, to his relief, that Lowell's buggy was gone. He tied his horse in front of the Nolan house, walked up the path, pleased to be back with good news for Shelby, keenly eager to see her again. He supposed he should knock, now that he no longer lived there, and did so. Mrs. Nolan came in response. He was astonished by the glacial set of her usually friendly face when she looked at him and said, "So you're back."

"That's pretty obvious," Hack said. "What isn't is what's the matter with you."

"Well, how do you expect us to feel, especially Mary?"

"Ma'am," Hack said, "I'd like to know more about this, and we could talk better indoors. Besides, I'd like to see Shelby, if she isn't mad about something, too."

She nodded, and he stepped in and followed her to the parlor.

"Now," he said, "I'd admire to know what you've got stuck in your craw."

"Don't play innocent, Hack Sumpter," she said tartly. "I never dreamed you and Jim could spread lies like that. Jim had a reason, seeing he never stood much chance against Spence. But what was your stake in it?"

"You seem to be talking about the

charges we made to the sheriff," Hack said, his own voice growing hot. "Lowell's competition for Mary had nothing to do with it. Two men tried to murder and rob Jim and me, and they were working for Spence Lowell. There were other things connected with Lowell I wanted the sheriff to investigate. He might have got somewhere if he hadn't been so plagued hard to get moving."

"So the men worked at the mine. Why did that make Spence guilty, too?"

"I'm convinced he is."

"You're convinced, without a speck of proof to convince anybody else. You understand this, Hack. We knew Spence years before we ever heard of you, or Jim, either. He won a fight that would have finished most men. It's sinful to malign a fellow like that, even if you were honestly mistaken."

"How'd you hear about it?"

"It's all over camp, I expect. And you and Jim must have spread it. Who else would?"

"So help me, we didn't."

"Hah," she said.

"Mary feels your way, too, huh?"

"Even more so."

"And Shelby?"

Mrs. Nolan looked away. "Well — she says she trusts your judgment, but God knows why she does."

"She's got better eyes than you have, Mrs. Nolan, even in her shape. Is she upstairs?"

At the woman's nod, Hack took his leave and ascended to the second floor. Shelby opened the door at his knock and stood impassive until he said, "Hello, partner."

"Hack!" she cried. She drew him into the room and shut the door. "How did it go?"

"Ticked off to a T. Fine steers and at our price. They'll be home in Black Canyon tomorrow night."

"Wonderful."

They sat down.

"Me and Jim seem to be in Dutch downstairs," Hack said.

Her face sobered. "It's hard to blame them, though, Hack. They've known Spence so long he's like one of the family to them."

"And they expect him to become more so."

"I don't know about Mary. Naturally her mother wants her to make a good marriage. They resent the rumors they think you started."

"Well, we didn't. We talked to the sheriff and nobody else. Do you know how the Nolans happened to hear of it?"

"Spence told Tom Gowan what you'd charged him with. Tom's a mutual friend. He told Mary, thinking she ought to know."

"Then it's not all over camp. It was just Lowell's way to queer Jim real good with Mary. He doesn't have the confidence in himself I thought he had."

"Do you think he told Tom just to get him to tell Mary?"

"I'd bet on it. It prepared her in case this thing really breaks into the open. It gets her on his side real early while horning Jim out."

"How did you connect it with Spence?"

He explained, and he saw the doubts leave her face as it grew sterner. "That means," she said, when he had finished, "that I was blinded by a man I considered a friend."

"Through a tool called Murname."

She lifted her head, her cheeks paling. "The man you killed?"

"Yes. Does it bother you that I killed him?"

She didn't answer directly, saying, "I supposed you couldn't help it."

So it did bother her, the same as it had helped turn Mary against him. She considered him hard and vengeful. He rose from his chair. At the door he said, "I reckon Jim had best stay away from here."

"Mary's very angry with you both."

When he reached the street, he thought of Lundy Imes, the little teamster who had befriended him so readily when he first reached Silver. He knew Lundy would be over at the teamster hangout called Dutch Nick's. He left the black where it was, walked down to the corner and turned left toward the swinging footbridge over the creek. There were only a few ramshackle dwellings on that side of the stream and a number of buildings used for other purposes. But Nick's place was handy to the wagonyard and stage barn and the boarding houses used by the horse people in and around Silver.

Lundy was playing cribbage with Nick, and the other patrons were involved in quiet card games of their own. Lundy climbed to his feet when he looked up to see Hack standing by the table.

"Look who's here," he said in his trumpet voice. "How was the trip, Hack?" He held out his hand.

"Just fine."

"So this is the new rancher," Nick said. He was a portly man with a longhorn mustache. He got heavily to his feet and shook hands when Lundy finished the introduction. He went shuffling in behind the bar and came back with glasses and a bottle of Irish whiskey. "Set down, Hack. A drummer give me this fancy booze, and I been saving it for a celebration."

Hack took a chair, although he did not intend to stay very long. They wanted to know all about the drive and the ranch for which the new cattle were headed. They had nothing to say about the charges against Lowell. Since Lundy had known the man as long as the Nolan women had, his friendliness seemed proof that there was no widespread gossip, which Hack didn't think Lowell would want. Lowell had known that Gowan would tell Mary but no one else, and that Mary and her mother would not gossip about it, either. That was what Hack had hoped to gain from seeing Lundy.

It was around ten o'clock when the door opened and Twitch Harper swaggered in, a handful of camp roughs trailing him. Hack saw by the expressions on their faces that Nick and Lundy had experienced the little man's company before. The party headed for the bar and lined up.

"Where's that fat Dutchman?" Harper demanded loudly. "A little service here, Dutchie!"

"By Gott!" Nick said explosively, "you can go somewhere else for your service, you little rowdy!"

Harper wheeled toward him, the annoying grin screwing his face out of shape. But his eyes, instead of finding Nick, centered on Hack and narrowed. "Well, if it ain't Sumpter again. Cowboy, how come you pick a old maids' home to cut loose your wolf in?"

Hack knew then that this was no chance encounter. Harper had made the rounds, looking for him. Mildly, he said, "Every man to his own taste, Harper. If this isn't to yours, Nick made a good suggestion. Follow it."

Harper's eyes rounded, then he stalked over to the table. He twitched a shoulder, and the men with him watched in intent silence. Apparently they had had advance ballyhoo on what the braggart intended to do when he made the contact.

"Heard you knew a pal of mine, Sumpter," Harper went on. "Heard you got real lucky the day he cashed his chips."

Lundy's eyes flashed. "If you mean Monk Murname, you never heard of him till you hit this camp. It just whetted your appetite for glory. Why don't you take that filed-up gun and get travelin' while your own luck's still holdin' up?"

"Why — you mouthy runt!"

Harper reached out as if to haul Lundy from his chair, but Hack surged to his feet. Before he had come to a full stand he found himself staring into the gun that had appeared in Harper's fist. The little man's hand had receded, dropped and come up filled so fast it had been impossible to follow. Harper grinned again, vanity naked and ugly on his face.

"Set down, Sumpter. I've taken over, and you ain't chief in these parts no more. You're goin' back to nursin' calves."

Hack's eyes were bleak. Although the style was different, he had figured Harper to be cut from the same bolt as Murname, but he had figured wrong. This was as deadly a viper as ever tramped the streets of Silver, and he had not drifted in by chance. He had hung around until finally he had made the contact that was his main business here, then had crowded it hard. He was putting up the front of a gun crazy kid, but there was more to it than that.

"Take that gun off me, Harper," Hack said.

"Or what?" Harper grinned. "Where's your'n, Sumpter? Scared to carry it? Scared your luck won't run so sweet the next time?"

"How much is he paying you for this?"

"Who?"

"The man who hired you to kill me."

Harper's eyes widened. He twitched a shoulder. "Kill you? Hell, how can I when you won't wear a gun?" He backed off. "Something stinks around here, boys. Let's get some fresh air."

He wheeled and led his admirers through the doorway into the night.

In a worried voice, Lundy said, "Hack, that fella's crazy."

"I don't think so."

"He don't aim to leave you be till you've showed fight."

"I don't aim to be around here."

"He'll find you. He's made his play. It don't matter much where he kills you, as long as he does."

"And maybe," Nick added somberly, "it don't matter to him how he does it. He thinks you got a crown that would look better on him."

Hack agreed that he would be crowded relentlessly until he had admitted cowardice or proved his courage. Some would see Harper as gun happy, others as a friend of Murname's, and nobody would connect him with Spence Lowell, who must have brought him here. . . .

Jim had rolled up his blankets but was awake when Hack came in from unsaddling and hobbling his horse. "How's Mary?" he asked.

"I didn't see her, Jim. My impression was that she went riding with Lowell. And I might as well tell you right off. He's boxed us in real good." Hack told him what the Nolans believed. "Guess I haven't helped you much, have I?"

Jim's voice hardened. "Forget it. I'm in this with you from here out."

eleven

The half-risen sun shafted a burning light across the rolling brown upland, and scented air stirred through the scattered juniper and the desiccated brush of the high desert. The steers were settled in their new location, and the night before Jim had said, "Why don't you take a couple of days and ride up to our southern range and get a look at it? I been there several times, and there's nothing I can't handle while you're gone. You won't need a camp outfit. Argent's only a day's ride, and you can put up there." The idea had appealed to Hack, and he had struck out at daybreak.

From Black Canyon south lay country he had never before entered. Stretching from Utah into Oregon, the strange land formation lay like a giant turtle between the Snake river in Idaho and the Humboldt in Nevada, ribbed here and there by short ranges of mountains and riven by deep trenched streams. There was less than a thousand herd of livestock in the hundred-fifty miles between the rivers, patched in only a few places by timber. Except for the breaks of the Owyhee and Bruneau and the mineral lodes that had given rise to mining camps, the plateau was made for ranching. Nobody had laid claim, as yet, to anything except around the edges. He and Jim had their range and their plan, and a deep obligation to Shelby for having made it possible.

The first day's riding showed him the sage plains Jim and Shelby had described and brought him to Argent. The camp, much newer than Silver City and still booming, sat on the backbone between the Snake and Owyhee rivers, another silver town identified by the stacks and tailing dumps that first came into sight on the monotonous horizon. Not a tree shaded its long, dusty street, which had a sleepy look Hack knew would vanish at sunset. There was a public corral on the near end of camp, and he put up the black and walked on to what looked like a fair hotel.

By the time he had bought his supper, a flaming sun had sunk to rest on the rimrock toward Oregon. The camp's eating and boarding houses were returning miners and mill hands to the street for the evening's diversions. Visitors threaded among them, bent on the business that had brought them to the camp. He saw three bold faced women turn into an establishment that, in spite of its frontier falsefront, called itself the Gay Paree.

He drifted along the street until darkness had driven everyone through some doorway, then walked toward his hotel, sufficiently worn by a day in the saddle to be ready for bed. Abruptly he hauled up to throw a quick, searching stare toward a man who had come out of a corner doorway on beyond the intersection ahead. The man looked across the dust into his eyes, then turned and walked off in the other direction, seeming to hurry.

Hack went thumping after him, yelling, "Dunn! Wait!"

The man stopped and swung around, and an awkward grin climbed into his ash-grey face as Hack came up to him. "Well," Dunn said sheepishly, "you're off your beat. Thought it was you, then guessed it wasn't. I don't see like I used to."

That was pretty feeble, and Hack knew he had tried to avoid him and slip away and was angered by it. "How long have you been here?" he said while they shook hands.

"Not long," Dunn said vaguely. "What're you doing up this way?"

"Seeing some country. You working here?"

Dunn nodded. "I was headin' for Pioche, then I run into a job here and took it for a spell. How about a drink?"

"Fine."

Dunn led the way to an offstreet establishment frequented by the camp's quieter element. They found a vacant table, then Dunn went to the bar and came back with a bottle of whiskey and two glasses. He sat down, and there was still a guilty look around his eyes.

"Dunn, why'd you do it?" Hack said.

Dunn looked startled. "Do what?"

"Pull out so sudden. It makes twice. I think I've got a right to an explanation . . ."

Dunn looked away. "I reckon you have. I ain't good for you, Hack."

"I'm not a kid anymore. But what made you say that?"

"I ain't what you think. We were good friends once, and that's what you remember and all you see. For one thing, I can't stay put. If you'd knocked around with me you'd soon have been a saddle bum, yourself."

"You could have let me choose."

Dunn shook his head. "Not at your age, then. You'd of throwed up everything and come along, when I left Iron Cross. I

165

didn't want to be responsible for that. So I went without telling you."

"And left Silver damned quick after I got there."

"Itchy feet again. That's all."

"And the next time I come through Argent, you'll be gone again."

"I couldn't promise you otherwise."

Hack's eyes were hard yet veiled with bewilderment. Dunn's aging had grown more plain in the elapsed weeks, he thought. Maybe he wasn't well. Whatever, it was time he was thinking about the day when he couldn't work anymore and would need a home and friends. Would he settle someplace then? Hack knew he would not. Dunn would keep wandering until the day he died.

Yet that did not explain his evasion in Silver, and Hack was determined to get to the bottom of it now. He said, "Dunn, you're still holding out. Why did you cut out of Silver just as fast?"

A pained look flicked in Dunn's eyes. "All right. Nobody there knows we used to be friends. The few times we talked a few minutes wouldn't mean otherwise."

"So?"

"I wanted to keep us strangers."

"But why?"

"To help you, maybe. I couldn't explain without admitting things I'm ashamed of. But I guess I'd better. I traveled with the wild bunch plenty in my time, Hack. Had before Iron Cross, knew I'd go back to it. It started from my being too good with a gun. That's why I told you I was sorry I'd taught you to shoot. Why I tried to talk you out of meeting Murname. I figured you'd probably take him, and I knew where it could lead."

"I told you he was sent to get me," Hack said impatiently. "Now there's another after me. Twitch Harper. Know him?"

Dunn's eyes narrowed. "He around?"

"Yeah. Claims to be a pal of Murname's. Pretends to be gun-happy and out to re-place me as Silver's top gun."

"He ain't a bluff."

"I know that. Somebody's paying him to kill me. But there's one thing I still don't get about you. You said you wanted to help me. How?"

Dunn shook his head doggedly. "Well, I don't want to raise your hopes. Figured to do what I could without you relyin' on it. Thought I'd fade a while, then try to get a job at the Big Casino."

"You know that's a bogus mine?"

"Not for sure, but I know enough I'd like

167

to learn more. Used to ride with a man who works there. Figured he might take me on. His name's Ed Pointer. Ever seen him?"

"Not to know it. What's he look like?"

"He ain't got much neck."

"I've seen him," Hack said excitedly. "He was with Murname when they bush-whacked me. So that's where he's been hiding. Do you know anything about Spence Lowell?"

Dunn shook his head. "Except what they say around Silver, which is all in his favor. Figured at first Ed and Monk pulled that job on their own hook. Then I got to wondering. Had a reason. A few years ago Pointer, Lacey and Yarbo hung out around the Comstock. They'd worked up a real slick scheme. They'd break into stamp mills at night and steal amalgam. I ought to know. I helped 'em with it quite a while. I guess you ain't been around mines much."

"No," Hack agreed.

"Well, amalgam's crude silver taken out of the ore and picked up in mercury in the stamp mills. When the mercury's burned off, the silver's molded into bullion for the mint. There's hundreds of mills in and around the Comstock, and it's funny about them. They'll watch their bullion like hawks, but they're plumb careless with the amalgam. Figure no common thief'd be able to refine and dispose of it, and they leave it on the tables at night and in containers in the smelter. Ed's outfit had only to break in and help themselves. Sometimes they picked up several thousand dollars' worth in one raid. And nobody ever got onto it that I ever heard."

"I'll be blamed," Hack said. "How did they burn off the quicksilver and get rid of so much bullion?"

Dunn leaned forward. "They had a fence, though I never learned who it was. I got paid my share in gold coin. After I come to Silver and learned they were respectable miners and heard that yarn about Lowell spending years redeeming a played out mine, I got to wondering. The Big Casino could finish the stuff and sell it to the mint. It didn't mean enough to me to do anything till you got involved. I wondered if Ed hadn't been workin' for Lowell all along. They must have kept that up two or three years and could have gathered a fortune."

"They were bringing it to the Big Casino," Hack said, "and storing it there. Lowell could have had other crews pulling the same thing in other mining countries. Since he had to wait for his return, he raised overhead money the way I lost mine. Now he's working the stuff and selling it as the product of his own mine."

"Whoa," Dunn said. "I'm not saying that's the case. It's just my notion."

It fit too well for Hack not to be convinced. He grinned. "There could be a million dollars' worth of the stuff stored there right now. That's the reason for the stockade and heavy guard and all the secrecy. Dunn, if we could persuade the sheriff to make an official search, we'd have them redhanded."

"How're you gonna persuade him?"

"If you know Pointer's bunch used to steal amalgam —"

"Don't forget," Dunn cut in, "that I used to steal it with them. And there's plenty more Pointer could spill about me if he wanted. I can't go to any sheriff, Hack. The most I can do is try to help you otherwise."

"When will you try to get in with Pointer again?"

"Pretty soon. He might wonder, if I hit him up for a job too soon after he got in trouble with you." Dunn wiped the flat of his hand over his mouth, shaking his head, wanting to do something but enormously handicapped by his own record. Abruptly he changed the subject. "Your best chance against Harper is to face him, like you did Murname. Otherwise, he'll have to dry gulch you. Which, if he hopes to be paid for it, he would."

"I know, but I had to kill one man that way, and I don't want to kill another."

"If you feel that way, there's no danger of you taking the wrong trail, like I did." Dunn rose to his feet. "Mebbe we've spent too much time together, already. Don't try to get hold of me. If I get anything for you, I'll get hold of you."

"Any reason why I shouldn't tell the sheriff what you've told if I keep my source a secret?"

"He wouldn't move against a man of Lowell's standing on hearsay, even if he believed you."

"But if I could get him to concede that I might be right, he'd act quicker when I can give him something solid."

"Suit yourself," Dunn said. He strode toward the door. Hack rode out of Argent at daylight, enheartened and yet depressed. All he had gained was a more lucid idea of what he faced and the hope that Dunn would find a way to help upset Lowell. Yet he still felt that it would be wise to tell the sheriff what he had learned. Gilpin did not deny that two of the men working for Lowell had been renegades all along. He had to be made to see the plausibility of his theory and the unlikelihood of Lowell's finding an honest bonanza in a long played out mine. Then he might open his eyes to other suspicious things, like the fence and guard and strict prohibition against any outsider going down in the Big Casino.

The downgrade ride went swiftly and, due to his early start, he reached Black Canyon before Jim had got back from outriding the cattle. He left a note for Jim and headed on for Silver, reaching there barely in time to catch Charlie Gilpin before he left his office for the day. Gilpin's blue eyes dropped instantly to the gun that rode Hack's hip.

"You loaded for bear?" he said.

Hack shook his head. "No, but I don't aim to let one corner me without the means to argue."

"I heard about Harper."

"I'm not looking for him. I come in to see you."

Gilpin's eyes focused to sharp points. "What, this time?"

Hack told him what he had learned from Dunn, withholding only Dunn's identity,

172

concluding, "I'm not asking you to do anything right now. Just open your mind and be ready when you've got reasons you can accept."

He thought Gilpin was somewhat impressed, although a cloudy skepticism still showed in his eyes. "Could you identify Pointer?"

"I'm sure of it," Hack said. "But I haven't seen him in camp or any of those around here."

"Come to think of it, neither have I, lately."

"So he could be laying low."

"I'll go along with that. He's off the bolt with Yarbo and Lacey. Maybe I'm being mighty bullheaded, Sumpter, but that still don't involve Lowell. What else do you intend to do about it?"

"Nothing, if they'll leave it that way, till I hear from my friend. I could jeopardize his life."

"The people around here won't leave you alone." Gilpin let out a tired breath. "They expect you to tangle with Harper. I hear he pulled on you and run off at the mouth real bad."

"I'm leaving the next play to him, too."

"He wants it, and the sports'll crowd both of you. I wonder why people are so damned blood thirsty. They'll promote a fight in which other people stand to be killed, just for the excitement. I guess it relieves the monotony of their own two-bit lives."

"What would you do about Harper, Gilpin?"

"I never killed a man except in the line of duty." Gilpin's eyes hardened. "On the other hand, nobody ever tried to kill me except on them same occasions."

"I never wanted the reputation I seem to have."

"But you can't shake it. It's a pity, too. Lundy Imes told me about the cattle you bought and that you hope to develop a winter market and mebbe show this country you've got brains as well as gun savvy. That's a good idea, and I hope you live to see it through."

Hack came onto a street grown sooty with twilight and was at once aware that his presence in town had been widely advertised. His mouth flattened as he walked to his horse, which stood at the tierail outside the courthouse.

Bales, the town marshal, stood there. He said, "Look, Sumpter, we don't want more trouble."

Hack stiffened, and his eyes drilled into

him. "Sound like you think I'm after it, Bales."

"No. But Harper's been told you're here and armed."

"You told him you don't want trouble?"

Bales shook his head. "Wouldn't do any good."

"Then why not lock him up?"

"He ain't done nothing I could do it on, or I sure would."

"Why don't you take his gun away from him?"

"We don't have a firearms ordinance. He's gun-crazy, Sumpter, but I don't think you are. Why don't you stay outta camp till he gets tired of it and drifts on?"

"He won't. But I don't figure on a thing but getting some supper and heading back to the ranch."

"Good." Bales' expression softened. "I never pegged you for a glory hunter, Sumpter. Hope you didn't get that idea."

"I didn't."

It was the same old Silver, come to the end of a working day. Along the street business men were anticipating the closing of their establishments and going home to their families. In the dwellings on the sides of the canyon families were bent on their placid routines. Nothing had ever made

175

them marked or outstanding. Gilpin had called their lives dull, but Hack envied them. They could look forward with a reasonable confidence that they would be let alone to live their own lives.

He rode down Jordan to a beanery where he had gotten good meals before, racked his horse and went inside. He had a steak and hash browns and a wedge of dried peach pie. He ate calmly, not thinking of anything in particular yet aware that something deep in his brain had turned very cold. Most of the others in the place were transients, which let him feel anonymous himself.

There was no feeling of surprise when he merged onto the street to find it cleared in his immediate block. He checked this briefly as he crossed the walk to the hitching rail, an aversive tingling in his back. Harper was somewhere near, though not yet detectable. He had started to unwrap the reins from the polished pole when a mocking voice called to him.

"Well, if it ain't Sumpter."

Hack turned his head.

Harper had stepped out of the recessed doorway of the building next to the eating house. Alone. Armed. Grinning. He had stopped again at the exact distance he wanted. His shoulder twitched. There was nothing but the pale street light on him, while Hack stood in the yellow square that fell from a restaurant window. Like Murname, Harper was trying for advantages.

Hack swung his body slowly but he said nothing. He knew that scores of eyes were watching from scattered points of vantage, that the town was caught in the grip of the moment that had closed in on him.

Harper's voice raked him again. "Taken to wearin' a shooting iron, I see. What for? Shootin' rabbits?"

"Supposing," Hack said softly, "that you fish or cut bait."

twelve

For a moment nothing but the sound of distantly clattering dishes fell across the silence. Then Harper laughed. "Me? I'm happy. Ain't you, Sumpter? Why not? Sore because a better man keeps runnin' you outta camp?"

"This is your chance, Harper. Take it, or I'm stepping across this horse and riding out."

Harper wanted to fire a defensive shot. It was the only way he could kill his man and evade a murder charge. He wasn't grinning suddenly. This opportunity, which had excited him, could be taken away from him by a swing of that tall body away from him and into the saddle. The body was already turning.

Hack had not shifted the position of his feet when he saw Harper's hand flash into action, produce a blob of rosy red and a roar that ripped open the silence. Something slammed into him as he shot back, just once, and the cold spot in his brain exploded, and the chill shot through his body. The black reared and snorted, pulling at its reins. Hack tried to grab the hitch rail for support with a hand that wouldn't move. He came down on his back, grunting, waiting for Harper's finishing shot.

It did not come. He shook his head and shoved up on the elbow of his good right arm, smelling the smoke that dribbled from his own pistol.

Harper was down, unmoving.

Hack rolled over, got to his knees then on to his feet. He staggered over to Harper, and there was a bloody spot in the center of the man's chest. Through the heart again, the way Dunn had taught him. Harper was fast, incredibly so, but he didn't know where a man's heart was located. Nor would he have hit it had it been to the left, as he supposed, for his bullet had slammed against the bone of the shoulder. Hack could not feel it yet. There was only blood and a paralyzed arm to tell him.

They began to emerge, the gallery, the excitement heated men of Silver. Bales came with them from the hazy distance. The marshal should have known that it was settled, but he hunkered and felt of Harper's wrist. He straightened and put a flat stare on Hack.

"I hope he done the reaching, Sumpter."

"He did," a voice assured him. "Me and Fred seen it from that step-back entrance, over there. Sumpter was starting to leave when Harper pulled. Ain't that right, Fred?"

"That's how it happened, Bales," a second voice responded. "The little reptile's trained lightning only got him killed, finally. That was a whale of a shot, Sumpter. Anybody that says you killed Murname by luck is clean crazy."

"Shut up," Hack said.

"You need a doctor," Bales said in a moderated voice.

"My horse —"

"Take it down to Sampson's, Fred," Bales said. "Sumpter won't be riding it right off with a busted shoulder. You look like you're coming apart, Sumpter. Can you make it to Doc Bethers?"

"Why not?"

Bethers still lived behind his office, and presently Hack found himself lying on the high, narrow table again, with the doctor using scissors to help get off his shirt. Bales was the only other one present. Hack refused an offer of whiskey before Bethers probed the wound, then poured the scalding disinfectant into it. He lay with gritted teeth while his shoulder was manipulated into the proper position.

The numbness started to wear off, and it became pure misery. He began to wonder why the marshal waited. Fred and his friend had cleared him, and there must have been other witnesses. Presently Bethers had him sit up, with his legs dangling over the edge of the table, while he finished strapping the shoulder.

"You'll have to stick around town a while," Bethers said. "You try riding with that broken shoulder and get spilled and you could cripple yourself for life. You understand that?"

Hack scowled. "How long?"

"Couple of weeks, and longer before you can ride very much."

Hack voiced his uneasiness, finally, "Gonna hold me, Bales?"'

"No," the marshal answered, "but I aim to help you get a room when doc's done with you. Where do you want to stay?"

"Eastman, I guess."

"It's up to the sheriff, but the inquest will likely be tomorrow. After that you might be held. It depends."

"I know."

When Bethers was finished, he said, "I'm getting tired of patching you up,

Sumpter. What gets you into so much trouble?"

"You tell me."

Bales walked to the hotel with him and didn't leave until Hack was in a rented room. Maybe he was relieved to have Harper off his hands, or maybe he had started to feel friendlier. Then the marshal scratched his head and said, "Don't take this wrong, Sumpter. But was I you, I'd try a change of pasture."

"Why?"

"I'd go where nobody knew me. If you don't —" Bales shrugged eloquently.

"There'll be another Harper along?" Hack said.

"Maybe a better man than Harper."

"Well, I like it here."

Bales sighed and left.

Hack removed the loose, bloody shirt he had worn over his shoulders and tossed it into a corner. He had trouble unbuckling his gun belt with one hand, and afterward he sat on the edge of the bed trying to pull off his boots. His shoulder was hot with pain now, and there was a hollow emptiness in his stomach.

Only that morning he had left Argent with no thought of ending the day in this place and condition. Jim would be worried, for he had said in the note that he would be back that night. What was worse, the herd and work would be up to Jim now for weeks. He would write a note, Hack decided, and hire somebody to take it out to Black Canyon.

And now Lowell and Pointer were up to Dunn. There was nothing he could do to help either friend when he could hardly move his body without being wrenched with pain. Dunn's only stake in it was friendship, and if Lowell grew suspicious of him, he was doomed. While the man who had started after Lowell, in the first place, sat helpless and useless in a hot hotel room.

He got his boots off finally, then slipped out of his trousers and stretched on the bed. The moment of violence came back to him, but his feeling for it now was only one of drained aversion. There would be another Harper, Bales had said, and maybe a man better than Harper. You kill the man who's going to kill you, Dunn had said back there on Iron Cross.

The inquest, held the next morning, was as cut and dried as the two previous ones had been. But he had grown even more notorious, for it was attended by every man in town who could get there. The testi-

183

mony was all in his favor again. Harper had laid his tongue on Sumpter in an intolerable way. Man after man attested to having heard his brags and threats. Finally he had been the one to seek Sumpter deliberately, and he had pulled his gun when Sumpter was turning away.

But it failed to erase the event from camp history. Hack was aware when he left the proceedings that, while they admired him in an awestruck way, his supporters had also grown afraid of him, themselves. Bales was friendly but, like the sheriff, clearly looked on him as a dangerous man whom violence followed and from whom it could lash out shatteringly. A man apart, now, a man to talk about but not to rub shoulders with, anymore. And he could not tell them yet what had been back of it all.

Even Lundy Imes seemed changed. The little teamster came to the hotel room that same evening. He was solicitous, perturbed and quiet. He wanted to do something, but all Hack had in mind was to get word out to Jim. Lundy knew a boy he could get to ride to Black Canyon and promised to do it the next day.

"I feel to blame," he said, "and Nick feels the same way."

"Why?" Hack said in surprise.

"Well, we both gave off head to that little reptile, the night he bullyragged you in Nick's place. If we'd kept shut, Harper might not have pushed it like he did."

"That made no difference. He was hired to kill me."

"Hired?" Lundy's eyes bugged. "Who by?"

"I'm not free to say, but it's something I sure hope to prove."

"In that case, whoever it was'll hire somebody else."

"It's likely."

"Who did you lock horns with, anyway?"

"Don't pry at me, Lundy."

Lundy lighted a stogie and took a turn around the room. "You tell the law about it?"

"I said don't pry."

Lundy looked at him, stung by the temper. "God, Hack, we're friends." Then he shrugged. "I know you're bound to be edgy a while. Forget it." He started toward the door.

"Wait," Hack said. "How do they feel about this down at the boarding house?"

"The Nolans? No use denying they figure you're a pretty rough hombre."

"Mostly, I meant Shelby."

"I haven't talked to her about it." Lundy

185

nodded and went out.

Hack sat down on the bed, feeling the things Dunn had talked about that started a man down the wrong trail. His temper seemed filed to a hair trigger. He had a haunting uneasiness he had not felt before. When a man killed another, whatever the cause, he destroyed a part of himself. If he found he liked the queer charge that came with it — well, he didn't have to worry about that. He wasn't drawn to it. He was thoroughly repelled.

thirteen

With her mother's help, Mary Nolan was cutting out a winter dress. Shelby sat in a chair by the dining room table, seeming to watch although all she could do was join in the small talk. Mary had her lips full of pins she was inserting in the tissue paper to tack it to the cloth, and her mother was puzzling over a complicated section of the pattern and muttering to herself. Mary heard the front screen door bang shut, and a moment later Lundy Imes came into the room where they were working.

"Hello, Lundy," Mary said around the pins in her lips.

"Oh, it's you, Lundy," Shelby said quickly. "How's Hack?"

"If you mean his bunged-up shoulder," Lundy said grumpily, "it's comin' along all right."

"Is something else wrong?" Shelby asked. Mary was surprised by the apprehension in her voice.

"Well, I hope it's his imagination," Lundy answered. "A man's pretty keyed up after what he's been through. But he's got the notion somebody hired Harper to kill him, that the bantam wasn't just another glory hunter the way everybody thought."

"Why, who'd do that?" Mary said, aghast.

"He wouldn't talk about it."

"He's excusing himself," Mrs. Nolan said flatly. "He's turned out to be a real troublemaker, and he only gets what he asks for."

Shelby turned an angry face toward her. "That's not so."

"Look at the talk they started about Spence," Mrs. Nolan retorted. "Now, I suppose, he's fixing to claim Spence hired Harper to do away with him."

"He's not trying to excuse himself," Shelby said. "He's not that way."

"No," Mrs. Nolan admitted. "He doesn't seem to care what people think of him."

"That isn't true, either, Mrs. Nolan."

Lundy went out again, and Mary felt a sudden indifference to the new dress. Her mother looked at her and after a moment cleared her throat. Mary paid her no attention but went back dutifully to pinning on the pattern. She was a little nervous, anyway. Spence had gone down to the railroad a few days ago and was supposed to get back that day, which meant she might see him this evening. She wasn't at all eager for that because, the night before he left, she had promised to marry him. She hadn't told her mother yet, nor Shelby. Her mother would approve highly, of course, but Shelby refused to share their anger against Jim and Hack for their wild charges against Spence.

Presently she said irritably, "Mother, let's do this some other time."

Her mother looked at her shrewdly. "It's your dress."

Mary went out to the porch and sat down, meaning to intercept Spence if he came by on his way home, as he probably would. The days were shortening, she noticed. It was only a little after six, yet there was scarcely an hour left of daylight.

She had been on the porch only a few minutes when Spence's saddler came around the bend of Washington Street. He saw her waiting for him and lifted a hand, smiling. He rode on to the path to the house, and he had some tightly rolled papers under his arm which he handled carefully while he swung out of the saddle. There was a sheen of excitement in his eyes, she noticed, as she watched him come up the walk toward her.

"Well, hello," she said, smiling, when he had mounted the steps.

"Good evening, Mary."

"Just getting back?"

"I stopped at the hotel to make myself presentable." He laughed lightly and caught her hands, his gaiety astonishing her.

She rose to her feet, uneasy about his kissing her there on the porch, although no one else was in view. But he did kiss her, insistently and lingeringly, then he picked up the roll he had put down on a chair.

"Guess what I've got to show you," he said. "It was at the post office when I got home."

"I have no idea."

He unrolled the papers and showed her, preliminary house plans from a San Francisco architect he said he had commissioned several weeks before. They were excellently conceived, she thought, extravagant but breathtaking. He explained them, feature by feature, all the things he had ordered for the house.

"It's far too fancy for this camp, Spence," she told him. "Your mine won't last forever. Neither will Silver City."

"It'll be in San Francisco," he said. "I've already bought the land. On Nob Hill, Mary."

"Why, Spence — will you be that rich?"

"We'll be able to afford it, my dear."

She had never seen him so boyishly excited, yet she could not blame him. He had planned a home such as the silver kings of the Comstock had built themselves in that exclusive section of the bay city. It was flattering that he wanted her to share it with him; Mary Nolan, daughter of a boarding house keeper, who had never known any place but this rough camp.

"When will you marry me?" he said urgently, for she had given him no date. "I've got to know now. I don't want to build this house unless you're going to live in it, too."

She looked away, then forced herself to meet his eyes. "When it's finished and we have a place to live."

"No, Mary. We'll go on a trip while we're waiting for it to be built."

"Can you leave the mine that long?"

"Everything's done now but to mine the ore we've blocked out. I've got good men who can see to that while I'm away. Later, I'll have to spend part of my time here, of course. You can come with me, when you like, and visit your old friends."

She was breathless, disconcerted, yet she knew it wasn't fair to stall him any longer when he had to commit himself to a huge expenditure on the house. "All right. A month from now," she agreed.

"That's too long."

"But there's so much to do to get ready."

"No. A week from now. Is that too soon for a man who's waited ten years?"

"The date's my privilege, Spence." She was surprised at the tartness in her voice.

Instantly contrite, he said, "I'm sorry. A month from today it is."

He wanted to go over the house plans again, every detail: the spacious entry hall with a domed ceiling and fine paneling of rare woods, the wide, winding stairs, the many bedrooms for their guests and children, the third floor ballroom, the enormous dining room, the library, the kitchen and servants' quarters. He couldn't get enough of it, yet she soon felt as if she had eaten too much rich food. She knew nothing of that kind of home, of the life they would lead there. It was beyond her grasp, so she could not feel it as strongly as he did, she supposed. She was relieved when he finally put the plans aside.

"What have you been doing?" he asked.

"Sewing a little. Did you hear about the gunfight?" It had happened while he was away.

His eyes sobered. "Fight? Who?"

"Hack Sumpter and a fellow they called Twitch Harper."

"Called?" Spence said sharply. "Harper's dead?"

"They buried him today. Why, what's so strange about that, Spence?"

"Nothing at all. I heard about Harper, and that they'd quarrelled or something. I just didn't expect Sumpter to kill him." He got to his feet, restless suddenly, puzzling her. "Well, I'd better get on to the mine. I'll see you soon." He kissed her briefly, went down to his horse and rode away.

So now there was a definite date on which she would change her whole way of life. She ought to be very excited, very uplifted about it and the kind of life that would open for her. She went into the house and on into the back parlor, to which her mother and Shelby had retired.

"I'm marrying Spence a month from today," she said.

An outright look of shock appeared on Shelby's face.

Smiling, her mother said, "Well, I'm glad you finally got down to brass tacks."

"You're happy about it, aren't you?"

"Of course. Aren't you?"

"Naturally. But I don't know if I want to be as rich as he'll be. I grew up in the

Owyhee and it's home to me. I don't know if I'll like living in San Francisco."

"San Francisco?"

"He's starting a big house on Nob Hill."

"Fancy that," her mother said in awe. "I never dreamed his prospects were that good."

"Mary," Shelby said suddenly, "I'd like to get out. Let's walk up to Shand's for sodas."

The idea appealed to Mary, too, because she was far more restless than she should be. She had been surprised when, of late, Shelby had started going around town with her frequently. She knew that it had resulted from Hack, that man of such contradictory traits.

She said, "I'd like to, Shelby."

"Would you care to join us, Mrs. Nolan?" Shelby asked politely.

"No thanks, Shelby. This is one day when I'm glad to take the load off my feet."

There was relief in the blind girl's face, and Mary knew the suggestion had been made because Shelby wanted to talk to her in privacy. They went to the confectionery store on Jordan Street and sat down at one of the little wire-legged tables and had the sodas. The place was nearly empty, so they lingered. Shelby was very grave and quiet.

Finally Mary gave her a crooked smile and said, "You weren't happy with my big news, were you?"

"I'm going to hurt your feelings, Mary. I'm horrified."

"Horrified?" Mary gasped.

"I'm not exaggerating."

Weakly, Mary said, "I realize that we disagree on what Hack and Jim spread around about Spence. But —"

"Wait." Shelby lifted a hand. "I'll talk. You'll listen. They spread nothing about Spence. They said some things to the sheriff but to nobody else. You've just assumed there's gossip about it. It was Tom Gowan who told you, and he said he learned it from Spence, himself. There's no evidence of it having gone any further."

"Saying such things to the sheriff was bad enough."

"No, Mary. Not when what they said is true. I don't hope to persuade you of that. We'll stick to your reasons for agreeing to marry him, finally. The big one is sympathy, which is a very bad substitute for love. Spence is very anxious to make it irrevocable before you realize that. Don't let it happen, Mary."

"Even if they're honestly mistaken about

it," Mary said desperately, "they did a vicious thing. I've known Spence so long. He couldn't be what they say. I think you're the one that's blind." She lifted her hand to her mouth, her cheeks staining. "I'm sorry. I only meant that — well, you're in love with Hack, aren't you?"

"Yes," Shelby said quietly.

"So you're the one who can't see things in their right perspective. Jim resents Spence's education and success. He wanted to queer him with me, so he swallowed what Hack claims."

"Oh, you idiot. It was Spence who feared Jim. Because of his youth and his manhood, which Spence lacks. He told Tom, knowing Tom would tell you. So who wanted to queer who?"

"You'll never make me believe that, Shelby."

"I guess not. So I'll add something to make it utterly preposterous. Spence Lowell is responsible for my blindness. He used a man named Murname, the first man Hack killed after Spence set him on him."

"So you're as distorted by hate as Hack is."

"He's not distorted nor malicious. He's not a killer. He's not violent by nature. He's the finest man I know."

"And Spence is the finest man I know. I want to marry him."

Shelby sighed and got some coins from her pocket and left them on the table. They walked out to the street, and Mary was physically dizzy from the shocking belief in Shelby's mind. The blind girl was resentful, Jim was jealous, and Hack was the friend of both of them.

"Let's walk a while," she said.

They turned west off Jordan starting up the hill, and there was nobody on the sidestreet walks. They went on to the uppermost street of Silver, where ran strings of old buildings, sheds and flimsy houses no longer in use. As they turned Mary saw the town lying below them, the cramped, noisy silver center where she had spent this much of her life, the cowtown into which it was changing.

Beyond the business streets in the bottom of the canyon, the better houses stepped in disorganized rows up the far slope. She had thought, she remembered, that Spence would build their house there. She wished it could be that way. It must be the thought of leaving here and striking off for far places, never to return except temporarily, that had upset her even before Shelby had spoken her mind.

They started back down the grade toward the business section. Shelby had had her say and was silent, her face still dark with her thoughts. They came onto Jordan Street and crossed and then dropped on down to Washington. Shelby stopped in the hallway to turn toward the stairs.

"It's off my conscience," she said. "If you do it anyway, it won't be that you weren't warned."

"I know you meant well, Shelby," Mary said gently. "But you're wrong, and time will prove it."

Shelby moved silently up the stairs.

Mary went on into the back parlor. Her mother was reading the paper, but she put it down. She said, "Have a nice walk?"

"Yes. We went up on the hill."

Mrs. Nolan sighed happily. "My, we'll have a lot to do. The wedding dress and all the new clothes you'll need for travelling. We'll have to get Miss Martingale to come in and help. We can't possibly do all that sewing, ourselves."

"Won't that keep till tomorrow?" Mary said wearily. Her mother's eyes rounded, then her mouth formed into a sympathetic smile. She said, "Honey, lots of girls get the willies just before they get married. The good ones."

"Fiddlesticks. I know the facts of life."

"Then what's ailing you?"

"I don't want to be married quite so soon."

"You're not going to postpone it?" her mother said uneasily.

"Of course not."

Mary went into her own room, undressed and slipped into bed. Her head ached and a tension down her back refused to yield to the comfort of the soft mattress. Nor would the oily, unwelcome thoughts stop slipping into her mind. Had Shelby succeeded in planting doubt, where Jim and Hack could not do it? She refused to entertain the possibility of her ever distrusting Spence herself.

She remembered when he had first come to live with them. She had been in pigtails and going to the public school up on the hill. He had been very good to her and especially understanding of the problems that had seemed so big to her then. Later, when he had been rich, she had been very proud that he still considered her a close friend. She hadn't remotely suspected an interest that eventually would become a desire to marry her. The fidelity in that, ever since she learned of it, had moved her deeply. There couldn't be a more patient or persistent man alive. She would not fail him now that there was a shadow on him, however flimsy it was.

Long later her mother came into the room on slow, heavy feet. She said, "I heard you tossing and turning," and sat down on the edge of the bed. Her hair was in braids, and she wore her nightgown. "Maybe I gave you the wrong impression. It isn't Spence's prospects. A mother wants to see her daughter safe in a good marriage, that's all. Spence'll give you that, and I was always uneasy about Jim, even before he did Spence dirt."

"Would you have wanted me to marry Spence when he seemed to be throwing his life and everything else down an apparently worthless mine?"

"If he could have taken care of you. Honey, you're mighty upset for a girl who's just picked her wedding day. If you're not sure —"

"I am sure," Mary said angrily. "Don't worry about it. I'll be all right tomorrow."

fourteen

The hole in his shoulder remained ringed with red and sometimes sent pain shooting in all directions, and the shattered bone maintained a dull and steady ache. Hack left the hotel each morning and made his way to Doc Bethers' office. The dressing changed and the shoulder rebound, he would come out on Washington again, feeling cramped and helpless with one arm lying uselessly in a sling and a mounting impatience crowding him. He was not used to inaction, and that in itself was hard enough to bear. He kept waiting for word from Dunn, on whom so much depended now, yet no word came. So the wearing days passed, each longer than a day had ever seemed to him.

Not the least reason for his dislike of the morning trips to the doctor was the fact that they brought him each time within shouting distance of the Nolan house. He had too much time to think, and more and more his mind built up the question of Shelby's reaction to the latest killing, since she had not liked the first one. He feared he had placed a new and insurmountable barrier between them, yet his desire to see her, to hear her voice and watch her smile was all the stronger.

More than once he had tried to screw up the courage to stop in and say hello and see if she had changed toward him like everyone else. Yet he always turned up to Jordan a block short of the Nolan house, and he could have been a thousand miles away from Shelby as far as anything but a business relationship was concerned. Things changed, that was all, and a man could not keep them from doing it.

He always hated to go back to the hotel to kill the long, unbearable hours. So usually he walked the length of Jordan and back before he gave it up and went to his room. The camp had its loafers whose roosts were soon apparent; on the benches in front of the saloons, certain street corners, the hitching rails on the shady side of the street that made leaning posts. They always saw him coming and grinned at him and asked how he was making out as he passed. Yet what they offered him was not friendship, anymore. He excited them, for he had faced situations they would be afraid to face, and he had done what they lacked the skill to do. He never stopped except to give curt answers as to his progress, and if they asked anything else his crankiness shut them up.

He had developed a wariness while on the street that he had never felt before, a steady watching for the new Murname or Harper or whatever the next one's name would be. It was not fear induced by the crippling wound, for he had shot Harper after he suffered it. The dreadful fact was that he was magnetized, drawing dangerous men toward him now, even if Lowell was left out of the equation.

Lundy had sent word to Jim, but it was not until the end of the second week that Jim found time to ride in to Silver. Hack was delighted to see him, but Jim had a grim look on his face that instantly sobered him.

"Something wrong out there?" he said.

"Not in Black Canyon."

"Where?"

Jim walked over and sat down on the bed, thumbing back his hat. "Well," he said in a worn voice, "I stopped in to see if I could make my peace with Mary. Pretty busy over there. Sewin'. Got a dressmaker in and everything."

"That doesn't sound alarming."

"They're sewin' a wedding dress."

"Lowell?"

"Well, she ain't standing up with me," Jim said. "Figured maybe you knew."

"I haven't even seen Lundy lately. God, Jim. It can't be."

"No. Not if I have to shoot the bastard in cold blood. It's to be right away, Hack. She better get her shock now than after she's married him, maybe brought a kid of his into the world." Jim managed to grin. "Well, I see the doc got you glued together again."

"Sort of. How're the steers?"

"Fat and sassy, and every head's answering roll call."

"I'm sorry I dumped everything onto your shoulders."

"You couldn't help it. How long will you be laid up?"

With a grimace, Hack said, "Doc says this rig's got to stay on another week. Says I can't ride much for quite a while afterwards, but the hell with that."

"Don't you rush it. A little patience now might save you a bum shoulder for life."

Reminded that Jim did not know why he had ridden up to the white sage plains, that day, only to be heard from next in Silver where he had killed a man, Hack explained. He summarized what he had learned from Dunn about Pointer's erstwhile activity in the theft of amalgam from the innumerable Nevada mills, and the probable fact that Lowell had been behind him, even then.

"So I come in to see the sheriff about it," he concluded, "hoping I could get him to open his mind. He concedes Pointer was in with Yarbo and Lacey, probably, but he still denies Lowell could have anything to do with it. So it's up to Dunn to keep Mary from making the misstep of her life."

"Can't say I'm hopeful."

"Me, either. But look here. You're not going out to the Big Casino with the idea of blowing Lowell's head off. Nothing's going to help Mary except her seeing the truth for herself."

Jim eyed him shrewdly. "All right. Now it's my turn. How come you've been steering clear of Shelby?"

"I figured she didn't like what I did. Did you see her?"

"Yeah. And the only thing she's put out about, that I could see, is you staying away so long. You get over and see her, and maybe I'll stay away from Lowell."

"You got a deal."

Jim left, and Hack decided that the longer he waited the harder it would be to comply with Jim's orders. He combed his hair and descended to the street, walking briskly down to Washington. Mary answered his knock and was less than enthusiastic about seeing him.

"Shelby's upstairs," she said.

Bluntly, he said, "I hear you're getting married."

She flushed. "So?"

"A man's supposed to wish you happiness, isn't he? And that I surely do."

"Thank you."

She turned and hurried off.

Maybe Shelby knew that a man's footsteps halting at her door would be his, since Jim had just left her. At least the door opened almost before he rapped the wood, and she said, "Hack?"

"Hello, Shelby," he said and entered the room, shutting the door behind him.

She stood as if taking an intent look at him. She said, "I didn't think you were so crippled you couldn't walk this far."

"I was afraid, Shelby. It's not a nice thing doing what I've had to do. It must look even worse to a woman."

"It looks to me like it does to you. Terrible. But you couldn't help it. Did you think I didn't know that?"

"Well —"

"Hey, come on." She smiled and stepped

206

toward him. "What happened to that confident man who wasn't going to recognize my not wanting him to like me? The man who made me do the things I feared, who was my eyes when we rode the range? The man who gave me back my life?"

He stared, astounded. He gasped, "Shelby —" then she was in his arms, her body clamped to his, her lips crushed to his hungry mouth. "You're not afraid of it now?" he said huskily.

"I'm only afraid of not getting you."

He knew that it was true, that he had stirred her out of the apathy of her disaster just as, in a single moment, she had lifted him from the depression that had been on him ever since the night he faced Harper. She had ripped away the sinister face the world had been showing him, wiped out his foreboding of doom.

"You'll come to the ranch?" he said. "We'll enlarge to make room for Jim. But you'll be the heart of it, Shelby, the reason for it, and, by God, I'll kill a dozen men if that many threaten our life together."

"Yes. We'll go out together when you're recovered. You'll have to be patient with me, but I'll learn. I'll make you a good wife."

"There's nothing you need to learn." He

watched her, amazed by the uplift of his spirits, the inspiration of energy and hope and fortitude following a near despair, all born of his restored confidence. It was a miracle-working change, one Shelby could use more of. Gently, he took her in his arms again, but instead of holding her to him he used his hands to untie the ribbon at the back of her head.

She jerked away. "What are you doing?"

"Then you do it."

"Do what?"

"Take off the mask."

"Oh, no." The words punched out at him as she stepped hastily free of his arms. "Maybe you don't mind the ugliness, but I do."

"As I love you, Shelby, there's nothing there but beauty. A true and wonderful beauty. Please."

Uncertainly she lifted her hands, and then the mask came off, and she stood like a statue that could not flinch under the impact of his inspection. There was nothing noticeable around her eyes now except the ghosts of her own terrible fear; time had erased the rest.

"I'd like to take a walk with you, Shelby," he said. "Right up the main street of Silver."

In a tired voice, she said, "Are you going to put me through another bad time like the day we were out at the ranch?"

"It helped you, didn't it?"

After a moment, she said very softly, "Yes. It did. I'll go with you, Hack."

They left the house without meeting anyone and came onto Washington and at the corner turned up to Jordan Street. Shelby walked with her head back, and he knew the courage it took, and the bright, busy street ran before them up the pitch of the canyon. The midafternoon sun struck them fully from in front and, to his surprise, she narrowed her eyelids.

"How much can you see?" he asked.

"Just the difference between light and dark. The sun's very bright, today, I take it."

"It is. And tell me. What did you do after Murname threw the lye at you?"

"Why, it was instinctive, I guess. The water pail was on the bench by the door just beside me. I stuck my head in it and kept it there as long as I could hold my breath, and I did that over and over. The doctors said it did a lot to minimize the damage."

They kept walking, and he said, "Maybe all the damage, except what's in your mind, Shelby. Fear can do terrible things. It can create the very conditions that horrify us, then seal us in 'em because we're afraid to try to break out."

"Fear?" she gasped. Then, a little stiffly, "I hadn't thought of myself as being cowardly."

"Sure not. Or you wouldn't be walking along the street without that useless mask and drawing admiring glances from every man who sees you."

"Do I really?" she said wistfully. "Do they look at my — eyes?"

"Naturally. The beautiful center of a lovely face."

"I halfway believe you. It — it could have cleared up by now, if it was going to."

"Shelby, it did."

"Honest Injun, Hack?"

"Honest Injun."

Her shoulders were a little squarer after that. For the first time since they left the house, she wore a smile. He could have proved what he said by strangers who would have no reason to lie if they were asked, but he wanted her to accept the truth from him, and he thought she was doing so, at least a little.

They walked to the upper end of the street, crossed over and came back along the opposite side. Then he took her back to the Nolan house.

"Was it as bad as the time I made you cook supper?" he asked, when they stopped on the porch.

"At first. I like it now, Hack. I really do."

"Will you throw away those masks?"

"Every one I own. I promise you."

He left her, then, and went back to his hotel.

That same evening, he got the mysterious message. He had gone out to eat his supper, and when he stopped to pick up his key on the way back the desk clerk said, "Wait a minute. You got a letter here, somewhere. The stage driver left it for you a while ago." He poked through some mail on a back ledge, then came over to the counter with a thin envelope addressed: Hack Sumpter, Eastman Hotel, Silver City. There was no postage stamp and no return address.

"Stage driver?" Hack said. It had not occurred to him to call at the post office on the improbable chance that he might receive mail.

He took the letter to his room to open it, and withdrew a single sheet of tablet paper. The writing was hard to decipher, but the message sent excitement charging through him: "Hack, I got to see you right away at the Ruby City hotel. I mean that right away. Tonight." There was no signature.

It must be from Dunn, who would not sign it for fear of its falling into the wrong hands. He had never seen Dunn's handwriting and could not verify it that way. It occurred to him that, if Dunn had roused suspicions at the Big Casino, this could be bait for a trap. Dunn had thought he was going back to Black Canyon. He wouldn't be apt to know he was staying in Silver temporarily, much less at what hotel. Hack took a turn around the floor, knowing he had to risk it.

His shell belt hung on the back of a chair, and he buckled it on with slow patience. He couldn't ride, but it was only a mile down to Ruby, and the walk would be good for him. He descended to the street, walked up to the bridge, and turned across the creek and down the long, dusky canyon.

The road had grown deserted, now that shadow deeply purpled the cleft, and the sun had dipped below War Eagle's feathery spine. He warmed to the walk and began to feel as good as he had before his injury. Just out of Ruby he stepped off the road while a freight outfit tooled past, a string of six teams pulling a highwheeler and a trail in from the railroad. He skirted the dust that hung behind it and went on, coming into Ruby and going at once to the battered hotel.

The letter had come from Dunn. He was registered under his own name and in a second floor room. Hack's hopes soared as he climbed the stairs.

Dunn answering his knock, said briefly, "Come in," and closed the door quickly after Hack had entered. He showed no surprise at seeing the sling, so he had learned what had happened since they saw each other last. Then his expression warmed a little, and he held out his hand.

"Set down," he said, nodding at the room's one chair. When Hack had taken it, he sat on the edge of the bed and began to roll a cigarette. He looked troubled and irritated and hesitant. He said, "I figured you never call for mail, so I gave the stage driver a dollar to take the letter to your hotel."

"Have you had any luck?"

"They gave me a job." Dunn's eyes came on him flatly. "I hired out to kill you. That's how I knew where to connect with you. They told me."

"You don't mean that."

The hard eyes were unblinking. "That's a fact. I waited a few days after I seen you in Argent, then drived over to the Big Casino. Pointer seemed glad enough to see me, but he said Lowell had gone down to the railroad and was the man that did the choosing. He let me put up there but sure seen to it that I didn't get a look at anything important. Nobody but the old hands get into the mine and mill. But I got a chance to learn one thing. What they're hauling to the stamp mill is waste rock. It sure ain't silver ore."

"That proves the mine is worthless, itself."

Nodding, Dunn said, "Yeah, but who's gonna catch 'em haulin' or crushing it? They can knock off anytime there's danger of being found out. The ore cars run on that high trestle, too high for visitors to see into, just to make it look like they're hoisting pay rock. I risked my life one night to take a look in the ore bin. That's how I found out. But getting down in the mine was too much for me. They never let me have that much time to myself."

Hack knew his restored hope was doomed to a short life. "When did Lowell get back?" he asked.

"Couple of days after you tangled with

Harper. He was plenty exercised about that. Harper was the only one they had with nerve enough to brace you, after what you done to Murname."

"Pointer knows you're a fast gun, then."

"Yeah. He sold Lowell the idea of sending me after you. Lowell figures it's worth a thousand dollars to see you dead. They had me wait long enough to have come from a long way off, then told me to get you."

"Pretending to be another glory hunter."

"They sure don't want me announcin' that I work for them."

"Well, what made you take it on?"

Dunn's eyes were unblinking. "Your life. If they didn't hire me, they'd send outside for somebody else. I can stall that a while, but not long. Then they'll see I'm stallin' to protect you."

"Think one of 'em could've seen me come here?"

Dunn shook his head. "As long as they trust me, they'll leave you to me. I told 'em it had to be that way, that I'd take care of you when, where and how I chose. But that's only good for two or three weeks at the most."

Bitterly, Hack said, "And I can't even use this bad arm for that long." He rose from the chair and paced restlessly.

"And he's never going to let up on you till you're dead." Dunn's mouth broke into a cold smile. "Was it me, I'd know when I was licked and I'd ride."

"You mean leave the country?"

"A man's business is to stay alive. When he's in a trap he can't shoot his way out of, he'd better run for it while he can. That ain't playin' the coward, Hack. It's being smart."

"Horsesweat. There's things better than staying alive. Like dying for what you think is right."

"Who knows what's right?"

"I know what I think is, and that's good enough."

Dunn shrugged. "Knew you'd feel that way. That's why we couldn't team up, Hack. I'd have liked to. I wanted to when I left the Iron Cross. So — well, I can cover you a while, but the way it is that's all I can do."

"It's all I ask. You going to stay here?"

"Mebbe, but don't try to see me again. It's too risky."

They shook hands and Hack walked out into the growing night.

Two deadlines confronted him. Very soon Mary would have joined her life to

Lowell's, and even before then Lowell might tumble to the fact that Dunn was stalling and hire another killer. Hack hated the prospect of another shootout as bad as he did the memory of the two that had gone before.

But there was still another approach to the problem: the amalgam, or an extraordinary quantity of bullion if they had converted it, that Lowell must have stored in the Big Casino. The sheriff and county prosecutor had to be convinced that it was there, to make a thorough legal search that would bring Lowell's house of cards tumbling down. There was now only one way of getting such evidence in time to save Mary. He would have to make the search himself. It would be an extremely dangerous undertaking, and he was still badly crippled, but there was no other way left to do it.

fifteen

He awakened early the next morning, turned restless by surging energies, and somehow managed to get through another long and wearing day. Preparing for what he proposed to undertake when night came again, he discarded the sling that had supported his arm and discovered that, except for soreness and the inevitable muscular weakening, he could use the arm and hand a little. The strapping that held the crippled shoulder rigid was hampering, but he had grown used to handling himself without using that arm very much.

Immediately after nightfall he slung his gunbelt in place and went down the back stairs of the hotel. The alley let him out on plunging South Street, and he was soon swallowed by the doors of Sampson's livery stable on Washington.

The black had been boarding there, idle, for over two weeks. While the hostler was saddling him, he said, "Sure you ain't rushing things, Sumpter? This fella's full of salt and vinegar. Should he dump you it could raise hell with that crippled wing."

"I'll risk it," Hack said. The man was curious as to his intentions, and he realized that it might be well to disguise them in case some of Lowell's men came around asking questions. He added, "I've got to get out to the ranch."

Gathering the reins in his weakened hand, he grasped the saddle horn with the other and swung up and across. It felt good to have leather between his knees again, and the horse was itching to go.

"Be back in two-three days," he told the stablehand and rode out into the street.

Silver's lights fell behind him, and the night swallowed him as he climbed the canyon toward its head. Off on either hand he could see the twinkling beacons of the few mines still pumping life into the camp. He passed the ghostly buildings of old Fairview and pressed on toward War Eagle's high summit, watching the stars come out in the sooty depths of the sky and feeling the cold of the autumn night deepen about him. He was gratified to find that riding did not pain him unduly. The black was frisky with pent-up energy but handled all right.

He thought of Mary and the fact that he was bent on destroying something that was precious to her, even if it was only an illusion created by an extremely clever man in

219

her mind. It was a sad necessity, one he was entering only in a spirit of inevitability, of fatedness. His calmness told him he had achieved something he had feared he might lack, the ability to control and direct the violent drives that could move him when he was pressed. He was glad of that for Shelby's sake. His love for her was the big and stabilizing fact of his life.

The south slope of the mountain was windy, and he regretted that he had not anticipated it and dressed warmly. The cold soaked into his bad shoulder and made it ache. Then, just beyond the junction of the Big Casino road and the turnoff trail to Black Canyon, he spied a rider ahead, coming toward him. A warning slid through him, and he wondered if he had been seen by the rider. He swung slowly off the road so as not to attract attention and then made for a brushy rock heap about a hundred feet away. It was downwind from the trail, which was why he had chosen it. He dismounted and stood with the black hidden, ready to quiet it and yet able to see a short stretch of the road.

About five minutes later the rider came by at an easy trot. It was Spence Lowell, on his way to pay his sleek, successful court to Mary. The black swung its head but made no betraying sound, and Lowell was again cut from sight. Hack stood there for some five minutes more, his lips pulled flat to his teeth. That was one of them out of his way, but Ed Pointer and his tough gang were bound to be at the mine.

He raised a vague huddle of buildings a few minutes later, seeing only a couple of lights that twinkled dimly across the dark distance from buildings higher than the stockade. He left the road immediately, dropping to the bottom of the gaping draw that wound down through the giant ground swells. The going was rough, and presently he swung down and began to lead the horse, which he wanted to get as close to the mine as he could. Once he barely missed stumbling into an old prospect hole, and again he had to climb the steep, rocky slope to get past a heap of rotting tailings. Yet he worked his way to within shouting distance of the mine yard before he left the horse tied in a clump of brush.

Five minutes later he reached the stockade fence, whose gate was shut, in which he hoped to find some kind of aperture he could slip through. There were only three sides to it, he remembered, set like a wide U against a sheer, rocky cliff on the east side. It took him fifteen minutes to discover that there was no such opening.

This would be no cinch. Even with two good arms his chances of climbing over into the yard were poor. The posts were cottonwood and juniper set deep in the ground and sharpened at the top. Possibly the fence was patrolled on the inside, as well. The bluff offered the only possible way in and, in the event he managed that, it posed a forbidding barrier to his getting away again with only one arm to help him climb out.

He hesitated for only a moment then made his slow, careful way to the horse. Mounting, he turned back along the draw until he could climb out on the east side and thus come in on top the bluff. Afterward he rode south again, presently reaching the lip of the rim above the mine. From that angle the drop-off looked even more alarming, but he dismounted and loosened the coiled rope thonged to his saddle.

He formed a loop in the rope and dropped it over an oblong rock wedged in a crevice. Testing, he found it secure enough to hold his weight. The other end of the rope lacked ten feet of reaching the ground below, but the ground at the foot of the bluff was piled with rubble. He twisted the rope around a leg to help brake, grasped it in his good hand and started.

He let himself descend only a foot or so at a time then stopped to keep the rope from burning him. Well before he was down he knew he would never get out that way. He came to the end of the rope, studied the talus below him and dropped free. Although he dug the edges of his boots into the mixture of rock and dirt, he overbalanced and rolled twice before he stopped. The hammering pain induced in his shoulder threatened to prove he had crowded his luck too hard already. He sat there pinching his lips, and finally the pain tapered off.

He was on the back side of the yard buildings, which was to his advantage. He climbed to his feet and made for the largest of them, which would be the main shaft house. It was dimly lighted, and he hoped that it was deserted for the night. The main shaft, itself, would be blocked by the hoisting cage, but every mine had to have an air and emergency shaft with ladders. He reached the back door of the building and found that they were placing their security reliance on the fence and guards in the yard. The door opened when he slid back the bar. A lantern hung on the far side of a big steam hoist that ran the cage. The boiler was off to the right, emitting the smells of a banked fire and warm grease and gently escaping steam. No one was in sight. He slipped in and closed the door behind him, shutting his eyes for a moment in relief.

The main shaft eye was blocked by the cage, as he had expected to find it, and he had to get down to the gallery of the first level at once. Tools and equipment were always left at these enlarged chambers, where the drifts joined the shaft, and once safely there he could risk lighting a lantern. There was an off chance that there would be a watchman inside the mine, but in view of their substantial outside precautions he doubted that.

The other shaft was at the far end of the long building, its eye fenced by bannisters, and the in-draft he noticed instantly told him that it helped to ventilate the subterranean levels. The opening was about three feet square, but cleats nailed to one side formed a ladder going down. He let himself quickly into the eye, feeling immediately an oppressive, trapped sensation wrought by the close confinement. He lowered himself clumsily for about fifty feet before he came out into the larger area of a drift, absolute darkness surrounding him.

For a moment he stood fighting panic,

completely in ignorance of the layout of the mine. He got on top the instinctive reaction and wet a finger to determine the direction of the air current he could still detect. The draft would be moving toward the main shaft and gallery, and his finger turned cold on the right side. He went to the left, groping along the cribbed walls of the drift and placing each footstep with care. If there was no gate at the main shaft, he could blunder into it and plunge to his death maybe a thousand feet deeper down.

He was warned that he had reached the gallery when the wall he followed receded suddenly from his touch. He struck a match, cupping the flame to keep the draft from extinguishing it. The gallery was not large, and he got his bearings in the brief moment of match light. He went on until he came to the far wall, where he had seen lanterns hanging. He took one down, raised the chimney then struck another match and lighted the lantern.

The flood of illumination dazzled but reassured him. A brief look about showed him that the gallery was walled. There were nails for hanging work garments, and he saw some rusty shovels, picks and drill steels. Somebody in the long ago had pasted theatrical posters on the bare spaces along the wall. Some were dancing girls in tights, each with a long-stockinged leg pointed upward, like a pump handle, and there was one of some trained dogs doing their tricks.

The framing of the lifting cage came down in the center, and the drift ran both ways, narrow car tracks snaking along its floor. The rails in both directions were dull colored and rusty, and he knew that this was one of the unproductive areas of the mine. In the other direction the car rails showed use. He saw that he had come in from a short cross-cut connecting with the air shaft.

He tipped the lantern light into the cage shaft to see that it ran down farther than the light would fall. The guide rails of the cage were shiny as far down as he could see, indicating that the present activity was centered in some level below him. There was no use spending time searching this level until he had investigated more likely areas, but he had to find a way to descend.

He turned into the drift on his left, walking between the rails of the car tracks. The smell of mustiness grew stronger, and water began to drip from the overhead surface. He wondered about the gas that formed in ancient workings and closely watched the flame of the lantern wick. As long as it burned normally, he could keep going.

He went on for a few hundred feet, jumping once when a rat appeared from somewhere, cut between his feet and went scurrying along the drift. Then he came to a crosscut traversing the drift and patiently followed it both ways to where it ended in rocky breasts. Returning to the drift, he pressed deeper into the darkness and eerie mystery.

The drift itself soon ended in a solid face, where a winze descended to the floor below. He spilled light into it, and the ladder looked rotten, with no bottom showing in the light. Yet he had no idea whether he could find another any better. He lowered himself into the winze and started down, the lantern clutched in his bad hand. It was slow, exhausting going, and it seemed forever before, wet with sweat, he dropped finally into the end of another drift.

This one showed no sign of recent activity, either, and the winze did not continue to let him go on down. The exertion and increasing underground temperature kept the sweat cracking onto his face as he moved along. Then he came into a sudden enlargement with ample signs of recent activity. He stepped around loose rock and tools littering the floor and stared along the glistening rails of the car tracks that ran on to the hoisting shaft. Studying the loose rock and the big chamber that contained it, he realized that this was where they were getting the supposed ore they were feeding through their bogus stamp mill. To cut down the expense of mining new rock, they were hoisting old waste that had been disposed of here years before.

He sat down on the rock; dizzy, the enormity of his undertaking enlarging as he considered it. There could be miles of these drifts and crosscuts in which he could become lost, to wander until exhaustion dropped him. Yet presently he climbed to his feet and followed the car tracks out to the main shaft gallery where he found a water barrel with a dipper hanging on a nail by it. He drank slowly, then sat down on an empty powder keg to rest again, weighted by a loneliness heavier than he had ever felt.

The descent to the next level, when finally he found a ladder, nearly exhausted him, and again panic began to eat away the drive of his will. The rotten mustiness of the air was the strongest he had encountered, and downfall warned that a caving process had begun. Yet he staggered on, hunting for the main gallery, which at last he found. It was empty, dank and stinking, and it began to dawn on him that this level was no longer being ventilated.

He wheeled and went over to the cage shaft, shining lantern light into it. The guide rails were heavily corroded with rust. The significance of that and the lack of ventilation wiped much of the discouragement from his mind. The cage was coming no farther down than the level above, from which they were hoisting the waste rock. That eliminated all the other levels, greatly reducing the area of his search.

He let out a gusty breath and realized that his head had started to ache. Turning, he walked back toward the ladder that had let him down. His heart began to hammer. Reaching the winze, he stared upward. He was tempted to discard the lantern and free both hands, but without it the darkness would be absolute and a misstep could be fatal. He clutched the bail in his teeth and started to climb, reaching out and lifting with his good arm and balancing himself with the other. The lantern chimney began to heat his shirt, threatening to burn him. He hooked it back on the elbow of his bad arm.

He barely made it to the next higher gallery, where again he went to the water barrel and drank and rested. He was still dizzy and slightly ill and, while he was in better air, he knew he had pressed his weakened body too hard. Yet he did not permit himself to remain motionless very long and pushed onto his feet again.

It took an eternity to go through that level, following to its end every drift and crosscut he found. Nowhere did he find signs of a hideout for the stolen amalgam or of the traffic there would have to be to and from it. He had it all to do over again on the level above, his last chance. After that there was only the comparatively short air shaft lifting to the surface. He found the ladder he had come down by and tackled the climb.

Now he could lift himself only a rung or so at each effort, then he had to stop and cling through moments while he caught his breath. His shoulder ached constantly, and he seemed to have no strength in that hand. When finally he crawled onto the floor of the drift above he could only lie there, his chest heaving, for a long while.

Finally he rose and walked toward the short crosscut leading to the air shaft, hoping the fresher air there would restore him. It was the first time he had been in it with a light. He noticed that the crosscut ran on for some twenty feet past the ventilating shaft, then was boarded up by ancient planks, probably to shut off some dangerous area. Then he stopped, staring at it as his numbed brain began to work. Could that be the hiding place? He walked on past the ladder to the wall and threw the lantern light onto it. There were narrow cracks between the planks, which were about a foot wide. He held the lantern close to a line of spikes and moved it slowly downward.

His heart started speeding in a wild, irrational excitement. The spikes in the lower two planks were old, but they had been struck recently by a hammer. He could get his finger ends behind the planks, but they were nailed solidly in position. Yet if the bottom ones were removed, a man could crawl under the others. Those two planks had been removed and replaced very recently, perhaps many times. He could have passed by his objective when he first entered the working levels of the mine.

He remembered the tools he had seen on this level and made his way back to the main gallery where he found a pinch bar. Returned to the wall, he stopped to consider the danger in what he was doing. He wondered if the light of his lantern reflected in the top of the air shaft. He was bound to make a racket when he prized off the planks. But he had to take the chance, for his hunch was strong that he was within feet of what he wanted.

The planks were stubborn and the rusty spikes screaked each time he managed to withdraw one slightly. Impatience goaded him, but each time he forced himself to wait while he listened carefully. He had the curled end of the bar under the bottom plank, and it took his full weight to budge it at all. He loosened one side a trifle, then went over to bring the other end even with it.

Suddenly he halted, his breath catching, certain he had heard a foreign sound. He crept back to the air shaft, leaving the lantern behind, and listened closely. Nothing happened, and he was about to return to his work when it came again from the shaft house above. From this closer position, the sound had a metallic ring. He let out a sigh when he realized that the wind had strengthened and was banging something around. He went back to the wall.

After the first plank, the other came off easily for he had more room to work in. He shoved the lantern through then crawled under, and there it was. Large granite buckets, each covered by a piece of canvas bound to the top, filled an area the size of a large room. The first one he uncovered showed him the glistening, silvery surface of amalgam.

This was the only thing worth having left in the mine, and the baffle furnace that burned away the quicksilver was the only productive piece of equipment in the mill. The fraud of it, which had given Lowell a heroic stature in most quarters, was appalling, even when the thefts and murders involved were disregarded.

And here was evidence to bring the man and his henchmen to the justice they had so cleverly cheated. Buried underground, surrounded by a stockade filled with deadly men. He decided that this chamber must have been the original chimney bonanza in the Big Casino, walled off finally as were numberless emptied treasure houses in a thousand mines. Then this one had been refilled with treasure of a different nature. Hack sat on his heels, fascinated by what he beheld, trying to estimate its worth. Certainly it could keep the mine paying handsomely for a long time to come. Whether it did or did not depended on him alone.

sixteen

Mary had expected Spence to call on her that night, and when he appeared, much later than was his habit, she found herself unaccountably annoyed. Her mother had gone to bed, Shelby was in her room, but instead of inviting Spence into the house, Mary felt an insistent resistance to him.

She stepped to the door, saying, "Let's sit out here."

She went over to the porch chairs and, puzzled, he followed. She accepted his kiss then sank into a chair, wondering why he had this wholly unexpected effect on her.

He was sensitive to her mood and, after looking at her closely, he said, "I'm sorry I'm so late. I had to ride down to Ruby to see a man tonight, so I thought I'd stop in on my way back. You look tired, Mary. Are you working too hard?"

"No." She watched him through the weak light, searching his indistinct face. She had placed him on the defensive, she realized. Instead of trying to jolly her into a lighter mood, he seemed to be setting himself for some kind of aggression from her. His features seemed as impenetrable as a casing of steel, and she had an odd sense of really seeing him for the first time. "Mother and Miss Martingale are doing all the sewing," she added. "About all I have to do is stand for fittings."

"I'd like to see your new clothes."

"In good time." She didn't want to talk about them or the wedding or pretentious house, and said quickly, "How's everything at the mine? Will you be able to get away?"

"Of course. Why?"

"I just asked. I'd like to go through it, sometime. I never have, you know. Why don't I? Tomorrow?"

He straightened in his chair. "For the same reason I haven't let anybody go down but my experienced men. I wasn't able to maintain it properly during the bad going. It's still very dangerous." His voice roughened. "You're upset. What's the matter?"

"I really don't know, except — well, would you mind if we didn't go on a wedding trip?"

"Why not?"

"I tell you, I don't know. Something about going so far away frightens me. I've worried about it."

He laughed. "We'd be safe enough. I'd

see to that. Where could we live here while waiting for the house?"

She knew then what she had really wanted to say. She had to say it. "I meant it might be better to wait till it's finished."

"Postpone the wedding? It might be next summer before the house is ready to occupy. We could put in the time travelling, enjoying ourselves."

"I'd like to wait, Spence. You asked what was troubling me, so I told you."

His reaction astonished her, for he sprang to his feet and stared down at her. "So you've succumbed to the lies Corbin and Sumpter spread about me," he breathed. "I never mentioned that matter to you, Mary. It seemed too ridiculous to dignify by taking it seriously."

"That has nothing to do with it, Spence —"

"Oh, doesn't it?" he retorted.

"No. It's my feeling for you. I guess I'm not as sure as I thought. I want to wait, Spence. You've got to accept that."

"So it's Corbin you want."

"If you insist on making an issue of it, maybe that's true."

He was making an effort to get hold of himself, and he bent to pick up his hat. "You're upset," he said. "And continuing this will only confuse matters. We'll talk about it when you're in a better frame of mind." He stared at her through a long moment, then turned and walked down to his horse. He rode south, vanishing into the night.

She sat inert and ill through a long moment, oblivious to the wind that had risen and turned the air uncomfortably cold, thinking of the violent, rancorous side he had showed her so unexpectedly. Something lay in his mind she had not suspected, and she had stirred it dangerously. Hack and Jim might not have been mistaken, and Spence himself had destroyed much of her belief that they were. It seemed to her now that there was something queer in his makeup, his fixation for a girl so young, his incredible tenacity in holding to his dream of success and wealth. A man like that might also see moral and ethical matters in a distorted light. He might dupe, steal and even kill in the service of his obsessive desires.

She rose and entered the house and mounted the stairs. She made her identifying tattoo on Shelby's door and stepped into her room. Shelby was whiling away the long hours by knitting, and she lifted her head.

"You were right," Mary said.

Shelby drew in a slow breath. "What opened your eyes?"

"Nothing. I just realized it. I turned to Spence in sympathy. It wore off."

"Oh. I thought —"

"The charges? They could be true. I don't know. But I do know I chose the wrong man."

"Have you told Spence?"

"Only that I wanted to wait till next spring. But I'm going to call the whole thing off."

"Thank heaven, Mary. Because he is guilty. He's going to be exposed, and you'd have been horribly hurt by that. And there's something else to consider. If you break it off, he'll hold Hack responsible. Hack ought to be warned. It's bound to bring on a crisis for him."

"You're right," Mary said in sudden worry. "He accused Hack and Jim, already. I'd better go over to the Eastman and see Hack. Want to come with me?"

"No, because you've got something to patch up with Hack. And Jim."

Mary walked up to Jordan Street, crossed and entered the lobby of the Eastman hotel. There was nobody in view, and she rang the little handbell that stood

238

on the desk. She knew old Purdy Allbright, who shuffled out of a doorway down the hall. She hurried toward him.

"I've got to see Hack Sumpter, Purdy," she said breathlessly. "What room's he in?"

"Don't know if he's there now, Mary, but his room's twenty-two, upstairs."

She thanked him and hurried up the narrow stairway, self-conscious about being there alone at night but determined to see Hack and warn him of possible trouble. The lamp that hung from the ceiling gave only a pale light to the upper hallway, but she found the door she wanted and knocked.

The door opened, and a man stood there whom she had never seen before. Her heart started to hammer. He was grey, and he had the coldest face she had ever seen, and he wore double guns.

"I'm sorry," she said in confusion. "I'm looking for Hack Sumpter. I must have —"
She glanced again at the room number on the door. It was the one Purdy had given her.

"Come in," he said. "I'm looking for Hack, myself." She wanted to turn and flee, but that was ridiculous. She stepped in, and he shut the door.

"Who are you?" she said.

"Dunn Hult."

"I'm Mary Nolan, a friend of his. I wonder where he is?"

"I dunno. I was waiting for him to get back."

"Have you looked in the saloons?"

He shook his head. "I sneaked into town and up the back stairs here, Miss Nolan. I'm not supposed to know him, let alone to be a friend of his. I been here quite a while."

Fear squirmed in her again. She doubted that Hack would have gone to one of the night places for diversion. He had kept strictly to himself ever since his fight with Harper.

"Anyhow, his gun's gone," Hult added.

"Oh, heavens." She knew she had to have help. "I'm afraid he's in danger, Mr. Hult. I may have worsened matters, and that's what I came to tell him."

There was a sharpening in the man's cold eyes. "Danger? How?"

"There's a man —"

"I know. Spence Lowell."

She stared, wide-eyed. "So you know about him."

"And I know him. He came down to Ruby tonight to see me."

"But why?"

"He thinks I'm going to kill Hack for him."

She could not stifle an outcry. "He hired you to do that tonight?" It was beyond belief. He couldn't have done anything so cold blooded, then come on to her house to see her.

"No, ma'am," Hult said. "That was earlier. Tonight he come to tell me to quit stalling and get the job done. That's what I sneaked up here to see Hack about. How do you come in?"

She told him in spilling words of the relationship between her and Spence and what had just transpired at her house.

"Well, that don't worry me as much," Hult said, "as what Hack's been up to all evening. He don't wear a gun unless he figures to need it. I taught him that, myself." He eyed her shrewdly. "That fella means something to you?"

"As a friend. He's interested in another girl, also a friend of mine. Everything he thinks about Spence Lowell's true, isn't it?"

"Does an honest man hire a killer?"

"And if he hired you, he hired Harper and probably Murname."

"No probable about it, ma'am. He did."

"His mine's a fake?"

"Yes. He's marketing bullion made from amalgam stole down in the Comstock.

241

He's paid the overhead by knockin' off cattlemen with beef money."

In a sick voice, she said, "Are you sure?"

"I once worked with a man of his. That's how come he hired me for this job."

"Why haven't you helped Hack by going to the sheriff, too?"

"Ma'am, if I testified against 'em, it would be against myself, as well."

She nodded. "I'm sorry. Do you suppose Hack went out to the mine to try to get evidence?"

"I'm afraid of it. And if Lowell went out there on the prod, I better not wait here for Hack. If he's there and falls into their hands, he's done for. I'm going out there."

"They might know at the livery where he went."

"I aim to check."

"I'll go down there with you."

They left the hotel room and tramped down the back stairs to the alleyway. Hult led her along the trashy passage until they came to the cross street. They walked openly down to Jordan, where he picked up the horse he had left at a hitch rack. He led the animal, and they went on to Washington. At the livery they learned that Hack had taken his horse out right after dark.

"I tried to talk him out of riding," the hostler said. "Mighty chancey with that game shoulder. But he said he had to go out to the ranch."

"Thank goodness," Mary breathed. "He's all right."

Hult's eyes beckoned her, and she followed him back to the street. He said, "I dunno. If he went to the mine, he'd have said something else in case he was checked on by one of them. And I don't think he'd go out to the ranch right now. He was relyin' on me digging up evidence at the Big Casino. I couldn't cut it, and only told him so last night. It's my hunch he went after it, himself. I'm going out to the mine, anyhow."

"And I'm going to the ranch to make sure."

She wasn't dressed for riding and lacked the time to change, so she asked the stableman to give her a fast horse with a side-saddle. In a few moments they were mounted and riding south. The men standing in knots along the street that led up the canyon turned to stare. It made her self-conscious, but Hult seemed indifferent to them, as coldly impersonal toward them as he seemed to be toward everything else. It was strange that she should be trusting herself to him in the night, a man she had never seen before, a two-gun, self-admitted outlaw himself.

They mounted the summit of War Eagle at a swift pace, and she felt the slope wind strengthen. As they dropped into the wild country beyond, she watched the stars that flung themselves in fiery brilliance across the sky. They came to the Black Canyon turnoff and reined in.

"If Hack's at the ranch," Hult said, "don't let him worry about me. I can go to the mine on some excuse, like tellin' 'em he seems to have left town. If he's not at the ranch, he's at the mine. In that case he'll need all the help he can get. Send Corbin in."

"All right."

She rode on at the same fast clip, the wind slowly chilling her yet not really aware of it because of the shock after shock she had absorbed that night. She reached the head of Black Canyon and, not long afterward, saw far below her the light of the little dugout on Axle Creek. She didn't slow the horse until she pulled it to a balled footed stop in front of the place.

The door swung open, and Jim stood there, staring out. "Mary!" he cried. "What's wrong?" He rushed out to her.

"Is Hack here?" she gasped.

"Hack? Of course not."

"Then he went to the mine," she said with a moan. She slid down from the saddle, and he took her indoors and freshened the fire while she told him in spilling words what had brought her.

Nodding, he said, "I'll be off, but you'd best stay here till morning. I'm going cross country, and I aim to travel."

"I can get back alone," she said. "Go on."

He hesitated. "This must be terrible for you."

"Not as bad as you think." She looked away. "You see, I'd realized my mistake, already."

He smiled, then his face set again as he buckled on his gun belt. She said "Good luck, Jim," and he went out into the night.

seventeen

Hack crawled under the partly dismantled wall that had concealed the stolen treasure and, on the other side, stood for a moment while he listened intently. Only the dead silence of the mine came back to him. He hurried down the crosscut to the main drift and turned on to the gallery at the hoisting shaft. It had occurred to him that a specimen taken from one of the pails holding that fabulous cache was all the proof he needed.

Every mineral region had its distinctive chemical characteristics, which experts could recognize, and Jim had told him that the Comstock ore, from which this amalgam had come, was much heavier in gold content than was the ore mined locally. An assayer could convince anybody that the Big Casino had not produced the bullion it was selling, including those with the staunchest faith in Spence Lowell.

He found pliers and with it removed the bullet from a shell he took from his belt, and he dumped out the powder. Then he hurried back to the cache, no longer feeling the weariness that had oppressed him so heavily. In a moment he had filled the empty cartridge with stolen amalgam and plugged it by replacing the bullet.

He put the cover back on the pail and looked around to make sure he had left no other evidence of his secret visit. Crawling out again, he hammered the planks back into place. Then he went back to the gallery with the bar he had used, blew out the lantern and replaced it on a hook. He stood motionless for a moment afterward while his eyes adjusted to the sudden blackness enfolding him. By then he was familiar with the ground he had to cover to get back to the air shaft, but he moved with caution until he was again at the foot of the ladder.

Looking upward, he could see a weak, reflected light from the lantern hanging in the shaft house. His ears made no report of movement up there except the occasional creaking caused by the persistent wind. He took a long breath and once more tackled a painful and wearing climb up the ladder. It went better than he had expected, for the distance was less than half of that between the mining levels. He stopped inside the eye of the shaft and again listened carefully.

He could still hear the plateau wind file

on the corner of the building, and somewhere nearby water dripped out a monotonous tinking. Yet he tensed uneasily as he made a last push with his legs that brought him onto the shaft house floor, ready for trouble if he met him there. Nothing happened. He slid on to the rear door by which he had entered and in a moment was outside. He would need all the wiliness and luck he could manage to get safely out of the fenced yard. He didn't even consider the rope by which he had let himself down the bluff. He would have to remove it, if he got away, but his horse was up there, and he could do that then.

He moved to the end of the building and followed the end wall to its far corner. The disordered jumble of the yard opened before him, buildings standing against the night, the cluttered connecting areas of ground. Two lighted structures were off to his left, probably the living quarters of Lowell and his henchmen. To the right was the gate, and he was surprised when he saw no one on guard there. It would be locked, then, but if they were relying on that alone he might be able to force it.

He made a swift run to the right, coming in behind a long rick of mine timbers. A moment later, when he was sure he had raised no alarm, he slipped onto the rear of the small building that stood just inside the gate. There was still nothing to worry him in the quiet sounds of the night. He moved around to the side of the shack and could almost touch the near end of the gate. It was built of slabwood. He could make out the chain that secured it.

Had he foreseen this, he would have brought a tool from the mine with which to force the lock. The best he could find, as it was, was a fist-sized stone, which he picked up. He would be in plain sight, when he worked at the lock, but he had to risk that. The chain made a turn around a post and was bolted to the gate on the other end. A padlock held the end links in its bite. He struck the lock a sharp blow with the rock without result. He could shatter it with one pistol shot, but that would be suicidal. Yet few such locks could stand hammering, and, holding it against the fence post, he struck it repeatedly. Finally it snapped open in his hand.

A driving urgency had built up in him, but he held himself to patience. He unwrapped the chain to get through, intending to replace it afterward and hoping he had not scuffed up the lock enough to attract attention. He swung the gate gently and froze on the spot when a fearful racket rent the silence.

He realized dismally that he had made his first wrong move. A bell loud as a fire alarm had been activated somewhere in the compound, battery powered and wired to be touched off if the gate was opened even enough for a man to slip through. He slid out through the opening, knowing there was no need to cover up now. He had jeopardized the whole undertaking for, to be on the safe side, they might take the amalgam out of the mine and hide it somewhere else.

Behind him men were running and shouting. He flung a glance at the cliff, but it was too high, all through here, for him to make his way directly to his horse. He plunged down into the brushy bottom of the ravine. Paused there, presently, he listened intently. Men had reached the gate and were talking excitedly, although he could not understand what they said. He hoped they would think that he had forced an entry, rather than made an escape, and was somewhere inside the yard. The talk up there broke off. He couldn't tell whether they were coming after him or going back to search the yard. The safer assumption was that they would do both. Swinging, he started moving along the draw.

He had to go back to where he had ridden onto the bench when he first arrived. He could detect no sound of pursuit and decided they had realized the hopelessness of searching the whole area surrounding the mine. He made his way onto the bench and turned south again, not hurrying for weariness had begun to mount in him once more. His discouragement enhanced it. Inconvenient though it might be for them, the amalgam thereafter would probably be kept in some remote place where it could not be tied to the Big Casino if discovered.

It took a long while to reach the place where he had left his horse. The black stood hipshot, tied to the stunted juniper where he had left it. Rock, between there and the edge of the rim, obstructed his view of the area below, and he moved through it for a look into the mine yard. He could see no movement down there at all.

Then a voice rapped out of the night.

"Get your hands up, Sumpter, and turn around!"

It was so unbelievable that he almost doubted his hearing. But the tone was in dead earnest, and he lifted his arms and turned. A stocky figure stood before him, having emerged from the rocks. A gun was

251

trained on him. In the dim light he seemed to have no neck.

"Pointer," Hack gasped.

The fellow laughed. "Wonderin' how we outguessed you? Easy, Sumpter. If you were outside, there was no use beating every sage bush around. If you'd been in and were tryin' to get out, it was a cinch you never come in through the gate. It had to be over the fence or down the bluff. We found your rope, and there was a quicker way for me to get up here than you took. I'll show you." Pointer moved in and took his gun and slid it under his own belt. "Get walking."

Hack's boots seemed full of lead, but there was no use crying over spilled milk. He had tried, and that was that. He followed Pointer's curt directions, retracing his own course for a short distance, then turning toward a notch that broke the edge of the rim. A man could gain footholds going down, he saw, and his captor told him to start. Each time he lowered himself, he noticed, Pointer waited until he was erect and a good target before he made his own descent. They came onto the bottom outside the fence, and Pointer directed him toward the gate. The man had a key he used to get them through, and that time the alarm did not go off.

"You got that bell trained?" Hack asked.

Pointer laughed. "I pulled a wire before I opened it." He reconnected it. "You're a pretty smart man, Sumpter, but not smart enough. You could have done the same."

"What comes next?"

"You're gonna keep us company a while. After that, who knows?"

They went on to the nearest structure showing light. "Open the door," Pointer said, "and go in." Hack pulled the latch and stepped into the room. Four hard cases sat there, regarding him with varying expressions, none of them friendly.

"So you took him," one of them drawled. "Who is he?"

"The bright Hack Sumpter," Pointer said.

Hack gave them a flat stare. He doubted that he was destined to live much longer, but they probably wanted to see Lowell before they wound it up, and Lowell had ridden in to Silver. Pointer shut the door, and the round face above his thick, short neck had a deceitful look of amiability.

"So you had a little tour of the works, eh, Sumpter. How do you like our mine?"

"How could a man get into it with a busted shoulder?" It was a feeble bluff, but the best Hack could do.

"Don't give me that. There's splinters knocked off the air shaft ladder. Somebody'd fooled around with some planks down there. We take precautions, Sumpter, like you found out. We always leave a horsehair hooked down there, to tell us if somebody's been prying."

"All right, that's quite a haul you've got. And no surprise to me."

"How'd you figure it out?"

Hack shrugged, knowing he dared not involve Dunn Hult. "I had plenty of time, sitting around getting over this little present from Twitch Harper."

"Well, you might as well set down again. You're gonna be here a while, likely permanent. There's a real deep water sump in the bottom of that main shaft."

"How many men have you dumped into it, already? Yarbo, I expect. And the wounded man I seen riding in here one time. Who was he?"

Pointer laughed. "What's the difference? But he never got shot raiding a stamp mill. We cut that out a couple of years ago. He got that little chunk of lead thrown his way by a gal's husband. She happened to be married to a real tough hombre. Our amigo figured he'd rather die with his boots on than his pants off and lit out for here." The humor was shallow, and ugly undercurrents were running in Pointer's mind.

Hack walked over to a bunk and seated himself. He could see no way out of this, and his fatigue had grown so heavy he was almost indifferent about it. Then the sound of distant hooffalls came through the walls of the shack and alerted the men watching him.

"That must be Spence," Pointer said. "Back earlier'n he said he'd be. Don't worry, Sumpter. He'll be right glad to see you here."

The horse stopped outside, and then the door sprang open and Lowell pushed in, a wild look on his face that energized Hack and surprised the others. When he noticed Hack, his eyes widened. "You! What're you doing here?"

"Prowling, Spence," Pointer explained. "But we caught him in time, and no harm's done."

"No harm?" Lowell's smokey eyes raked his hirelings. He walked toward Hack. "You son of a bitch," he breathed.

Hack surged to his feet, but Lowell's fist drove out and sledged him in the bad shoulder. The blow rocked him back, and the pain turned him sick.

"You — cheap counterfeit," he returned.

"Something jump the track in Silver, Spence?" Pointer said worriedly.

Lowell ignored him, his burning eyes riveted to Hack's. That was answer enough for Pointer, since they were in command here.

After a noisy intake of breath, Lowell said, "So you finally queered me with the one woman I ever cared for. I'll make you pay for it, Sumpter, and pay high."

"So you cared for the girl," Hack said.

"More than life itself."

"Don't give me that. Looks like she gave you no choice. But I reckon that if you had one between her and your illgotten gains you wouldn't hesitate. You couldn't love anybody, Lowell. You wanted her youth and beauty to grace the other enviable assets you've been accumulating."

"Twist that bad arm behind him, Ed," Lowell said harshly. "Twist it till it breaks again."

"Now, look here," Pointer said. "What's the need of that?"

"The need's inside of Lowell," Hack said. "He can't stand to lose. You ought to know, Pointer. Look at the way he made a worthless hole in the ground look like a good mine. I don't know what happened between you and your intended, Lowell.

But I never talked to her about you in my life. Consider this. Once a person takes a good look at you, there's quite a lot that seems fishy. Maybe she just took a good look."

"Is that all that's wrong down there?" Pointer said insistently. "If we're up against something, Spence, you better calm down and tell us."

"If she's grown suspicious," Lowell returned, "what's to keep the sheriff from it?"

"Particularly," Hack said, "if I disappear."

"We can handle it," Pointer said with confidence. "Simmer down, Spence. Forget about your precious reputation. What good'll it do you if your girl's already given you the gate? Let them prove their case. Sumpter's the only one besides us that's been down in the mine. He ain't gonna tell anybody what he seen down there."

"If I just drop out of sight," Hack put in, "Gilpin'll be out here with a search warrant to fine comb your mine."

"We'll move the stuff and let him prove we had anything to do with you."

"Where's he going to see any pay ore in that mine?"

"We'll find a way around that, Sumpter. Don't bother yourself with our worries.

You've got your own."

Lowell nodded. "All right. You could deny me beauty, Sumpter, but you can't deny me treasure. So I'll content myself with the treasure."

"There might not even be that," Pointer said impatiently, "if we don't get moving. Pete, build up your steam, pronto. We're gonna need the slip to move the stuff. Sid, you and Ace take Sumpter down in the mine and —"

Lowell's hand cut him off. "I'll take care of Sumpter, myself. My way. Slow and hard."

"We're gonna need all hands."

"Tie him to a chair till we're done. I want to take my time with him."

A man pulled Hack off the bunk and shoved him into a chair. They used a rope to lash him there, and saw to it that the knots were well beyond the reach of his hands. They went out, Lowell last, and he shut the door behind him. He locked it from the outside.

Hack wasted no strength against his bindings, but sat numbly, looking around. The room offered nothing with which to cut himself loose, even if he could get it. It was apparently the main bunkhouse and, besides the bed, it held a minimum of furnishings. In the long ago somebody had pasted newspaper on the walls, which shrunken boards had cracked at every seam. Cobwebs hung from the rafters, and a piece of tin roofing fluttered in the wind. The dusty windows looked like painted black squares, trembling in their frames.

They would move the loot deep into the mine, he supposed, into an unventilated and caving area where a searcher would not venture. That would take them several hours, then he would find out what special torture Lowell had in mind before murdering him.

The racket that broke loose made him jerk against his bindings. It was the alarm bell which, he realized, was on the outside wall of this building. Somebody else had forced the gate who did not know about the wire that had to be pulled. In a moment shots struck across the night in a staccato burst, down toward the gate. He heard a man's high-pitched yell. Only a few moments had passed since Pointer took his crew into the mine. Whoever had come in was in serious trouble.

The shooting stopped with an intensity of silence that created a vacuum in his ears in which he could hear the heavy pounding of his blood. A moment later somebody tried the door. Another shot rang out, shattering the lock. The door opened, and Dunn Hult stood there, a smoking gun in each hand. His eyes were squinted against the light, having difficulty in focusing.

"Here, Dunn!" Hack called.

Dunn staggered as he came forward. The front of his shirt was bloody, and there was a claylike color on his face. His opaque eyes flattened on the figure in the chair and flickered in recognition. Then he made a choked sound and sagged to his knees, shaking his head.

"Figured this was where they'd have you," he said, coughing. "That damned bell. I cleared the yard, Hack, but there's more of 'em comin' outta the mine."

He dragged himself over the planks, coming in behind the chair while Hack watched with stunned eyes. In a moment the rope loosened, and he worked out of it speedily. Dunn had slumped on the floor behind the chair. Hack dropped to his knees. The back of Dunn's shirt was bloody, too. He was hit hard.

"Get goin'," Dunn gasped.

"I'm taking you or staying."

"Too late —"

A lifeless wrist confirmed that. Dunn had taken his last lonely ride.

eighteen

One of Dunn's guns had caught under his body, the other lay where it had dropped from his relaxed hand. Hack took both and filled them from Dunn's belt to conserve his own ammunition. Maybe Dunn had given him more than a chance to fight for his life. The cartridge filled with stolen amalgam was still in his own belt, and they hadn't even suspected it. Somehow he had to get away alive with it. He stepped out into the restored calm of the night.

Nothing happened in the second in which he was framed in the lighted doorway, so nobody was watching the building. The men who had come up from the second level of the mine did not know, then, just what had broken loose up here. The light in the bunkhouse might delude them into thinking that he was still there helpless. But they would be hunting the intruder. He faded into the shadow beside the building, seeking a plan. If he could get to the gate and slip through, he could make for the place where he had come down the bluff ahead of Pointer and reach his horse.

He went farther down the slope toward the lower fence and, cut from view of the main yard, moved quickly until he had come behind the stamp mill. Nothing warned him of activity anywhere near him, and he pressed on, reaching the far corner of the building. He could not see the gate from there so began to work his way upgrade again. From the upper corner the gate was in view and it was shut, with two men standing there watchfully.

He remained still for a long moment, fighting a desire to rush them and take his chances, which would be very slim when he had no idea of how many others were somewhere close, ready to cut him down on sight. If he could find a length of rope, he might be able to scale the stockade fence, and a good place to try it would be in the deep shadows behind the stamp mill. He had never determined where they kept their horses and where it should be easy to find rope. It would probably be one of the old buildings down on the south edge of the yard.

He moved along the back of the mill again, then pressed on behind the main bunkhouse. He was about to go farther on when he froze in his tracks, staring forward. Two more men were coming along the fence toward him. He ducked back into cover. They were guarding the gate and patrolling the inside of the fence to make sure the intruder did not escape. They could find and deal with him at leisure.

There was one remaining chance, the tramway that jutted over the wall by which waste was dumped onto the heap in the ravine below. There was no trestle work on the outside to let him down, but a free drop to the tailings would be easier on him than falling into their hands again. To get onto the tramway he would have to enter the shaft house and risk blundering into somebody lingering there to keep the intruder from seeking refuge in the depths of the mine. Getting across the yard to the structure would be dangerous, itself.

He let the patrol pass him then moved along the fence in the opposite direction. His eyes bored through the dim starlight ahead to warn him if he met more men coming on. The big building on the south side proved to be the stable, and he slid into it, still wanting rope to let himself down outside the fence if he could get onto the tramway.

From the breathing, stamping and warmth of the interior it was evident that there were a number of horses in here, although he could hardly see his hand in front of him. He waited through several moments to adjust to the deeper darkness, but it did little good. He could tell that he was in the main aisle of the barn, and he crept forward until he came to the big rollback door on the yard side. He eased it open very slowly, watching the yard.

In the improved light he could see several saddles hung over a pole. None of them had an attached rope, for these were not cowhands. There were half a dozen horses beyond the manger that ran down one side of the aisle. He decided to take their halter ropes and piece them together, letting the animals mill loose in the barn.

A better idea replaced that while he moved toward the manger. If he could stampede them through the yard, he could utterly confuse the situation for his enemies and in it try to rush the gate. He untied the horses one by one, not bothering to take their ropes, then opened the end door that gave access to these stalls. He let the animals out, removed his hat and began to fan them while he yelled at the top of his lungs.

The results were all he hoped for. The horses, none of them sufficiently exercised, broke away from each other in snorting confusion and went pounding across the yard in all directions. He fired two shots into the air to encourage them in it, vaguely hearing shouts that were all but drowned in the din. He saw two men running across the yard toward him and quickly turned back through the barn and out its back door. Thereafter he headed toward the rear of the shaft house, using such cover as he found in the yard, the hoof hammering of the horses still coming to him from several directions and accompanied by their panicked whistling.

He did not enter the shaft house and, instead, moved down along its north wall to a point where he could see the main gate. The eruption of bedlam action had drawn the two men he had seen there previously away from it. He ran to the rear of the gateside shack, and at the same time a man loomed across the way, staring at him. He motioned at the figure and pointed toward the back corner of the stamp mill. The man accepted him for the gate guard and moved down toward the mill obediently.

"You damned idiot!" somebody yelled. "That's him by the gate!"

Hack wheeled and saw Spence Lowell over at the front door of the shaft house.

The other man swung around just as Lowell fired from his position. Hack shot at the red burst of flame, and Lowell ducked into cover. The other man heeled around and bolted in the same direction. Hack slid back to the gate and came up short. Ed Pointer stood between the wall of the shack there and the fence. In the second of discovery, Pointer shot pointblank.

Hack threw himself aside, driving his own shot into the echo of Pointer's. He shot again before Pointer could repeat, and the man went down in a forward pitch and lay still.

They had cut into him again from the shaft house, driving him away from the gate and into the shelter in which lay Pointer's body. They would cover the gate thereafter, he realized, and he could not get onto the tramway to try that escape with them where they were.

Lowell's voice fell across the silence. "Sumpter's loose, boys! There're two of them to watch out for!"

The man had recognized him and did not realize that the new intruder was dead. That gave them something of the handicap weighing on him, forcing them to proceed with caution. Gambling that they were intent on the gate, he bent and made a run along the fence, reached the side of the shaft house safely and went around to the rear. He came face to face with a man and nearly shot before he recognized him.

He breathed, "Jim!"

He saw the other figure relax, and they moved toward each other. "How in tunket?" Hack began in a whisper, but Jim simply pointed toward the bluff. He had come in the same way Hack had, using his rope to let himself down.

"Mary came after me," he whispered, "and I cut a fast beeline crosscountry for here."

"She believes us now?"

"She believes us."

"It's easier getting in. We've got to shoot our way out of here."

Jim nodded. "How do we tackle it?"

"Lowell's inside this building with at least one other. They think I'm nailed down at the gate. Let's go through the back and try to take 'em."

"You know the layout. Lead on."

The men inside had blown out the lantern that had hung there earlier. Hack placed his steps cautiously as he moved in through the back opening, Jim on his left side. A man stood on either side of the far door, watching out into the yard.

"Drop your guns!" Hack shouted. "Or

we'll cut you down!"

They swung shooting. Hack fired, hearing Jim's gun roar in his ear. One of them staggered into the full light of the doorway and dropped. The other man yelled.

"I'm quittin'!"

Hack heard his gun clatter on the floor and went forward, jamming his own gun into the fellow's stomach. The man who had fallen was unstirring and he wasn't Spence Lowell.

"Where's Lowell?" he demanded.

"Dead," the man gasped. "You hit him in the yard, a while ago. He made it in here but didn't last five minutes. He's over by the shaft cage."

"That's right," Jim called. "I see him."

"So's Ed Pointer," Hack told his prisoner. "Yell to your amigos to come in with their hands up, or you're dead, too, and so are they."

The man started yelling.

Charlie Gilpin had a wry look on his face when he glanced up at the visitor who had just entered his office. "Dunno if I want to talk to the man," he said, "who gave me the reddest face I've had in all my years in office."

"Well, don't worry about it," Hack said. "Spence Lowell had a lot of you oldtimers fooled. It took an outsider to see into him, I guess. What did the assayer say about my sample?"

"What you predicted. On top of that, the men you brought in tried to outdo each other spilling what they knew in hopes of getting off easier."

"Has the amalgam been impounded?"

Gilpin nodded. "That and the gold in Lowell's safe. The mill operators that lost the amalgam weren't even aware of it. The county attorney says they couldn't enter a claim, since they can't estimate what they were out, if any at all, or when they lost it. He says people like you and Shelby, who can make a bonafide claim, will collect. The balance'll go to the state like an un-claimed estate, he thinks."

"Well, I'm glad some of us can get our dues. At first that was all I was after. Later, there were other issues."

"I know," Gilpin agreed. "I'm sure glad Mary got her eyes open in time. Figure she and Jim can get together now?"

"Bound to."

"When're you going back to the ranch?"

"Depends on how soon Doc Bethers'll let me. I'm going over to see him next."

Bethers was in his office, momentarily idle, and sat with his feet cocked on his desk and a cigar in his mouth. Around the cigar, he said, "What've you been doing to Shelby?"

"You seen her?"

"This morning, on the street with Mrs. Nolan, proud and pretty as you please. I think you're responsible, but I don't know how you did it. I've tried ever since she got back to Silver to get her to throw away those damned masks."

Hack forgot that he had come in hoping to get the doctor's permission to return to the ranch. "Doc, what's her chances of seeing again, at least a little bit?"

Bethers removed the cigar and studied it. "I'd say they're good, now that she seems to believe she wasn't disfigured permanently. A woman's appearance is a mighty vital thing, Hack. It affects her whole outlook."

"But her eyesight, Doc? That's even more important."

Bethers shook his head. "Not till now, in Shelby's case. She's been afraid she'd see how horrible she looks and how everyone has lied to her about it. Fortunately, she had the presence of mind to dilute that lye solution when it hit her and do it fast. So the damage really wasn't deep, with most of it confined to the flesh around the eyes and to her mental makeup."

"But she's blind."

The doctor sighed. "I could be wrong, but I've had a feeling it's what we call hysterical blindness. She was a beautiful girl, as she still is, with a natural pride in that and hopes of love and marriage. So she was afraid she'd see beyond doubt that she looks as bad as she's imagined, and the blindness guaranteed that she never would have that crushing experience."

"Yeah," Hack agreed. "It makes sense."

Bethers eyed him owlishly. "Now she has the love and seems to have grown convinced that she isn't maimed. She could recover her sight if my theory's right, and if so it could be sudden. Some moment of great need to see or even of a strong wish to do so."

"Thanks, Doc," Hack said, turning toward the door.

"What'd you come in for?"

"It'll keep."

He reached the Nolan house in long strides and took the stairs two steps at a time. He had trouble waiting for Shelby to open her door, and the moment he was in her room he guided her across to her dresser.

"We're standing in front of your mirror," he said. "Looking into it. Shelby and Hack, and, if I do say it, we make a mighty handsome couple."

"I wish I could see," she said plaintively.

"Why don't you?"

"Don't be silly."

"Are you afraid of that mirror, Shelby?"

"Afraid? Not anymore. I hadn't realized it, though, till this moment."

"You don't think I've lied to you?"

"You wouldn't, Hack. I know that now."

"Then you're afraid of what I'd look like. Who told you about the crooked nose and buck teeth?"

Her mouth dropped open. She swung and lifted her face, and her eyes moved over his as realistically as if she were studying each detail. Then all at once she lifted her hand to her mouth. "Hack — I can see you — a little. I can make out the shape of your head."

Gently, he said, "It's because you want to, Shelby. That's all it takes. From light to shapes, then pretty soon the details." He bent his head toward her and knew he was right, that Bethers was right, when her mouth formed itself to receive his kiss.